THE NEW ADVENTURES OF SUPERMAN

HEAT WAVE

M. J. FRIEDMAN

BBC BOOKS

Published in the UK by BBC Books
a division of BBC Worldwide Publishing Ltd
Woodlands, 80 Wood Lane
London W12 0TT

First published 1996

ISBN 0 563 40472 8

Typeset by BBC Books
Printed and bound in Great Britain
by Clays Ltd, St Ives plc.

For Jerry Siegel and Joe Shuster

Acknowledgments

The author would like to recognize the efforts of Jerry Novick, without whose hard work and diligence this book would not have been possible. Thanks are also due to Mike Carlin, KC Carlson, Mike McAvennie, Dean Motter, and Lee Nordling at DC Comics, for invaluable noodling. Finally, the author would like to express his gratitude to Charles Kochman, Ann Goetz, and Scott Sonneborn—for giving me this project in the first place, and for displaying exemplary dedication and care throughout the course of the creative process.

PROLOGUE

It was hot. *Really* hot. But Colin Dunn couldn't think about that now. He could only run as fast as his legs might carry him through the dense, sun-streaked forest.

Finally, plunging into the clearing beyond, Colin stumbled on an exposed root and sprawled face first onto the grass ahead of him. Spurred by the rising thunder of approaching motorcycle engines, he tried to scramble to his feet.

"Come on!" screamed his redheaded companion, who had rushed past and then stopped to look back at him. Her eyes widened with fright as she glanced past Colin at their pursuers. "Please, they're right behind us!"

But it was too late. Before Colin knew it, they were surrounded by a pack of motorcycle thugs—big, burly men on huge, smoke-belching bikes, with metal limbs to replace the parts they'd lost in battle and evil intent in their slitted eyes.

As the robo-bikers rode circles around them, Colin grimaced at the strong scent of sweat and motor oil. Cackles of unholy joy assaulted his ears, sending iced water down his spine.

His companion clutched at his bare arm, squeezing it tightly enough to leave finger marks. "I told you so," she groaned. "I told you we should never have come here."

"You should have listened to the wench," bellowed Griffin, a seventeen-stone greasy mammoth of a man, over the roar of the circling motorcycles. He wiped the perspiration from his brow with a metal hand. "No one enters the Dragons' forest without an invite. Isn't that right, *compadres*?"

Griffin fashioned a toothy grin as his half dozen leather-clad followers rumbled in agreement. Each Dragon brandished a club, a chain, or a stout metal cudgel. And each one looked eager to demonstrate what happened to trespassers.

Abruptly Colin's eyes were drawn to a streak of red and blue in the sky. For a moment he saw the streak slow down, so that it was visible as a caped figure—one who was perhaps curious as to what was going on below.

Then the figure sped up again as it continued its flight, vanishing over the treetops that loomed all around. Colin grunted. He and his companion were on their own.

Spying a dead branch near his feet, Colin clutched at it and held it out like a weapon. Someone had to try to defend them—and it looked like it would have to be him.

"You jerks b-better stay back," Colin stammered at Griffin and his posse. But that only drew a round of jeers from the robo-bikers.

"Lookit him, Griff!" shouted Screech, the Dragons' second-in-command. He wiped a drip of sweat from his chin, an artificial eye shining

8

like a beacon. "He thinks he's some kind o' knight in shinin' armor."

Griffin sneered at Colin. "You're in no position to threaten anyone, little man. Stick or no stick, we're going to show you why they call this Dragon country."

He nudged his bike to the left, coming a little closer. The others followed suit, tightening the circle.

But before he could take a swipe at Colin, another voice rang out in the clearing. "As usual, Griffin, you've opened your mouth and inserted your big, smelly boot before gathering all the facts."

Griffin and his Dragons stopped dead in their tracks, turning to stare dumbfounded at the edge of the clearing. A lone figure separated himself from the trees—a tall, muscular figure on a sleek, black bike, with a grin on his masked face and a glint in his steely blue eyes.

"From over here," the newcomer went on, "the kid looks like he'd make fine knight material. And as for there being no help for him in this forest . . . well, as usual, you've forgotten about me."

Colin grinned through his perspiration. There was only one man who would pit himself against a ring of motorcycle heathens to save a couple of strangers.

"Bolt!" roared Griffin, his face twisting with anger. "You meddler! I'll mow you down and smash your bike into spare parts!"

Griffin revved the engine of his motorcycle, lowered his steel cudgel like a lance, and without hesitation shot off across the clearing. Bolt squinted at him, causing the tattooed snake on his right cheek to coil.

Then, sweeping his cloak behind his back, the hero lowered his staff and, revving his own bike, sped off across the clearing toward what would certainly be a thunderous clash.

The distance between them closed. One hundred feet apart, eighty, fifty, twenty. The two adversaries came ever closer, each bracing himself for the shattering impact to come.

Suddenly, with a horrifying squeal, the front wheel of Bolt's bike locked up. The startling loss of mobility had an instantaneous effect on the motorcycle's rider, throwing him headlong over the handlebars and through the air.

Before Colin knew it, Bolt had hit the ground with a sickening crunch. When he stopped rolling, he was clutching his right leg below the knee.

"Ahhh! My leg! My leg!" he cried.

Everyone rushed over to him—from Colin and his companion to Griffin and his Dragons to several of the people who'd been standing around, watching the scene being filmed. As they crowded around the screaming man, another voice raised itself above the din—that of the movie's director.

"Cut!" cried Dorian Hatch, rising from his seat. He was a stocky man in his late thirties, his dark hair pulled back into a fashionably tight ponytail. "What the hell is going on here?"

It wasn't really a question, Colin knew. Dorian Hatch didn't ask questions. He only gave orders.

As Hatch threw his rolled-up script on the ground, another man approached him. The second man—Beau Paris—was taller than the director by half a head, with curly blond hair and tanned good looks.

"I'll tell you what's going on!" railed Paris, the star of the film. "My stuntman just broke his leg. And if I'd decided to do my own stunt, like I usually do, that would've been *me* squirming on the ground out there!"

"I've heard this before," said Hatch, frowning. "'Someone's out to get me, Dorian. Someone's trying to sabotage the film.'"

The director dabbed at his forehead with a red bandanna. Like everyone else, thought Colin, Hatch was annoyed by the heat.

"But no one's out to get anyone, Beau," the director continued. "This was just another accident. And I'm not going to suspend shooting because of your paranoia."

"Dorian's right," said Arlee Atkinson, the beautiful redhead who had played Colin's companion. As soon as she was close enough, she took Dorian's arm. "They were just

11

accidents," she told Paris. "We'll get past them."

"Just accidents?" repeated the actor. He glared at Arlee.

"That's right," she said. "The two of you are just letting this heat wave get to you. You need to cool off."

"I'll cool off when this albatross of a film is over," Paris sneered. "And the way things are going, that may be sooner than expected—which'll be fine with me."

Hatch's eyes blazed. "It'll be over when *I* say it's over," he spat. "And not a second before."

Then, with Arlee Atkinson in tow, he stalked off. Paris watched them go, his mouth twisted in anger.

Colin shook his head. It had all sounded so good to him in the beginning—getting the chance to act in a Dorian Hatch epic, maybe the biggest of them all.

Now everything was going up in smoke.

CHAPTER ONE

As Lois Lane emerged from the subway, she paused just long enough to assess her reflection in the window of Dacy's department store. She had put her dark hair up, worn a miniskirt and a low-cut blouse, even dispensed with nylons, all in an effort to dress for the weather.

But it wasn't doing much good, the journalist thought as she resumed her slow, measured journey over the steaming sidewalks. She was careful not to move too quickly lest she raise her body temperature even a millionth of a degree.

So were all the other pedestrians on Seventh Avenue. The heat wave that had gripped the city seven days ago had made "record temperatures" a daily occurrence—and, unfortunately, rising tempers as well.

Lois herself wasn't angry with anyone, of course. Well, maybe *one* person—the WGBS weatherman who'd predicted a cooler summer than usual.

Oh, and whoever had decided Dacy's didn't need bigger awnings over their display windows. As it was, there was barely a strip of cooling shadow alongside the building.

Looking up at the digital sign in front of Metropolis First Federal Savings & Loan, Lois sighed heavily. Not even five minutes past nine, and it was already one hundred and two degrees.

13

When is this planet going to move a little further away from the sun? she thought with a sigh. Abruptly, she found herself smiling.

Planet, she mused. As in *Daily Planet*.

The very thought of it was nirvana. Just two more blocks, she told herself, and I'll be inside the *Daily Planet* Building, soaking up all that wonderful air-conditioning. That is, if I don't melt like the Wicked Witch of the West first.

It only took a few minutes to get there, thanks to the weaving technique she'd developed as a reporter and longtime Metropolis pedestrian. But by the time she came within fainting distance of the *Planet* building, her blouse was soaked and loose strands of hair stuck to her forehead. Her feet felt as if she'd been walking over hot coals. In short, she was a mess.

"This is the glamorous superjournalist for the *Daily Planet*?" she grunted out loud. Passing by a bank window, she stole another look at her reflection—and immediately regretted it. "I look more like a wet rat."

Just a few feet away from the *Planet*'s revolving door, Lois heard a by-now-familiar murmur running through the assembled masses. Looking up instinctively, she saw a red and blue streak make its way past the golden globe in front of the *Planet* building.

Forgetting the heat for a moment, she began to chuckle. "Look! Up in the sky," she said to nobody in particular. "It's a bird, it's a plane. No, it's . . ."

My fiancé, she added silently.

Lois gave a small wave to Superman. Spotting her, he slowed his flight momentarily and dipped down until he was skimming the air just above the pedestrians' heads, his red cape fluttering behind him.

She smiled at him. He smiled back, his blue eyes playful beneath his neat black hair—though, of course, no one but Lois knew he was smiling at *her*.

That was their secret. Or anyway, one of their secrets.

Superman then increased his speed and soared out of sight, leaving in his wake a cool breeze that gave momentary relief to those below him. Clark should be at work, Lois thought, as she pushed through the revolving doors into the *Planet*'s air-conditioned lobby. I wonder where he was flying off to.

Hurtling high above the city he was sworn to protect, all Superman could think about was impending disaster. He would have liked to linger a bit longer with Lois, but his super-hearing had picked up the makings of a tragedy. According to a radio newsman, a water main had broken at the intersection of Ninth and Bessolo.

At the corner of Ninth and Chesterfield, Superman plunged past several weary, sweating

15

commuters into the tiled confinement of a subway station. The Man of Steel had no time to explain his haste—only to veer right and plunge into the echoing darkness of the tunnel where the trains ran.

The rush of water from the broken sewer pipe would flood the Ninth Avenue line within seconds. The subway conductors would get word of it soon.

But that wouldn't help the 9:13. It would come roaring through the tunnel at any minute, its driver unaware of the flood that awaited him. The result? Derailment, destruction, and probably death.

That is, unless someone did something, and fast—someone who had been born on another planet and had powers and abilities far beyond those of other men.

Someone like *him*.

Pouring on the speed, Superman negotiated one dizzying bend in the tunnel after the other, moving faster than any train ever could. The 9:13 would come plowing into the flood in a matter of seconds—twenty, if he was lucky.

He had to be there first.

A moment later, Superman heard the creak and rattle of metal wheels against metal tracks. He saw the distant glare of sparks off the electrified third rail, which supplied the train's power.

In the middle ground, maybe fifty yards in front of the train, water was spewing out from a side tunnel onto the tracks in a frothy gush. Striking the opposite wall, the flood turned back on itself, creating the kind of eddy a whitewater rafter would have nightmares about.

Gritting his teeth, the Man of Steel sliced through the watery chaos and braced himself for what came next. As the train came thundering around a bend, he slowed down just enough to avoid damaging it.

Then he set his hands against the front of the lead car and applied a level of strength only he could muster. As he fought to slow the lead car's progress, Superman could see the shock and amazement on the driver's face.

Wheels shrieked. Sparks flew. But bit by bit, the train was slowing down. Glancing over his shoulder, Superman saw that they were painfully close to the rush of water.

Bringing all his power to bear, he brought the train to a screaming, grinding halt. A moment later, all he could hear was the pounding of the water in the tunnel behind him.

How about that? he thought. I really *am* more powerful than a speeding locomotive.

Looking at the conductor, he asked, "Are you all right?"

The man nodded, still open-mouthed with awe over what he had seen.

So far so good, thought Superman. But what about all the other people on the train?

Flying through the narrow space between the

cars and the tunnel walls, he peeked in through the train windows. A quick inspection showed him that none of the passengers had been hurt. In fact, no one even seemed to realize the magnitude of the danger they had been in. And by the time they did, the police would be here with rescue teams.

Superman was inclined to linger—to help with the rescue effort. But with Metropolis's heat wave going full blast, a new emergency seemed to crop up every few minutes.

He had barely completed that thought when he heard a scream. It was pretty far away, but that didn't mean anything to Superman. If he could hear it, he was on it.

Speeding past the train through the subway tunnel, he headed for Hob's Bay.

Tony Bonelli had never been so hot in his life. Neither had his three sons, or his wife, or the rest of their neighborhood.

Bad enough they had to live in a section of Metropolis other people called Suicide Slum. Bad enough he had to look out his window at broken-down cars, scattered refuse, and the occasional homeless person. He had learned to live with all that.

But when it got so hot you could burn your feet on the sidewalk, something had to be done about it. And Tony knew what to do. After all, he had grown up here in Hob's Bay. And nobody knew how to open a fire hydrant like he did.

Giving the thing one last tug with his oversized wrench, he released a jet of water that nearly reached the other side of the street. A moment later, Tony's kids were running in and out of the cold spray. And before long, the neighbors' kids had joined in, too.

Tony smiled. It looked like it wasn't going to be such a bad day after all.

Veering south toward Hob's Bay, Superman made a low sweep through Suicide Slum. That was where the scream had originated.

Suddenly, he heard it again—this time louder and more shrill than before. The Man of Steel shot straight up into the sky, twisted ever so slightly to change his trajectory, and headed down at breakneck speed toward the source of the cries.

It was only after he had arrived that he realized what was happening.

It was just a child, screaming with laughter as he played in the stream of water from an open fire hydrant. And he wasn't the only one. It looked like the whole neighborhood was taking turns cooling off.

Unfortunately, this kind of thing wasn't doing the city's water pressure any good. With a busted main back at Ninth and Bessolo, the city needed all the pressure it could get. If a fire broke out...

"Hey look!" a woman cried out. She pointed

to Superman, who was descending among them.

"It's Superman! Way cool!" shouted a red-haired boy in his early teens.

Landing on the sun-baked asphalt of the street below, Superman thought for a moment. He couldn't let the hydrant stay open, but by the same token, he couldn't leave these people high and dry.

Seeking out an adult, he put his hand on the man's shoulder. "Y'know," he said, "I think I've got a better way for you guys to cool off. Shut off the valve, I'll be right back."

The man grinned. "Whatever you say, Superman. Your word's good enough for Tony Bonelli."

The Man of Steel smiled. Then, gathering up his cape in one hand, he took off again into the sky. The wash of his passage rippled the surface of the puddles left in the street.

Superman returned a few minutes later with a titanic stack of abandoned tyres he'd collected. Descending to earth, he carefully deposited the tyres on the sidewalk. Then he turned his attention to the vacant lot across the street from the fire hydrant.

With steely eyed purpose, moving so fast it must have looked as if there were a dozen heroes and not one, the Man of Steel scooped out a huge, round hole in the ground. To his eye, it looked four feet deep and ten feet across.

That done, he streaked over to where he had

left the pile of tyres and picked them all up in one big bundle. Dropping them into the hole, Superman then focused his heat-vision into a wide beam.

With a concentrated burst, he melted the rubber of the tyres until it lined the entire hole, side to side. Then, moving his hands at superspeed, he applied the molten rubber to the sides as well. Finally, hovering above it, he cooled the smoking goo with a few blasts of his breath.

When he was finished, the reshaped rubber lined the hole so perfectly that not one bit of dirt showed through. But that was only the first part of his undertaking.

Weaving his way among the run-down edifices of Hob's Bay, Superman found an old, empty water tower that he'd noticed earlier. Fortunately, the thing was still in reasonably good repair.

Positioning himself underneath it, he flexed his muscles and raised it off its support structure. Then he headed for the bay, where he scooped up several hundred gallons of water.

It was a lot heavier now, and a lot more awkward—but nothing he couldn't handle. With a little extra speed, he returned to the site of his construction project.

By then, the whole neighborhood had turned out to see what was going on. Some police were there as well.

Slowing down above the hole, Superman tilted the water tower, allowing its cool contents to cascade into the makeshift pool. After the last drop had trickled out, he temporarily put the tower aside.

"There you go," he announced. "Hob's Bay Community Pool is now open."

The kids gathered around him and cheered. Tony clapped him on the shoulder.

"You done good," he said.

"Thanks," Superman replied.

Then he picked up the empty water tower and took off into the sky. It took only a couple of minutes for him to put it back where he'd found it and resecure its supports.

Just as he finished, he heard the whistle blow on the 9:30 ferry as it left the harbor.

Oh no, he thought. I'd better step on it. Otherwise Clark Kent is going to be late for another staff meeting.

CHAPTER TWO

Lois felt the scrutiny of her editor in chief, Perry White—not to mention the half dozen other staffers who'd assembled in the conference room for the day's morning meeting.

"Lois," said Perry, "where in the world is Clark?"

Unable to help it, Lois squirmed a bit in her chair. She had been politely trying to maintain the charade that she and her fiancé had agreed upon—that while on the job, professionalism came before romance.

Still, there wasn't a soul in the newsroom who didn't know that the two were romantically entwined.

She shrugged. "Sorry, Perry. He said he had some errands to run last night. I haven't seen him since we left work yesterday."

"Yeah," said one of her colleagues, half seriously. "Is she her partner's keeper?"

Perry glared at the one who'd spoken. "She's the closest thing to it. And since I can't ask Clark himself . . ."

Exasperated, he took a deep breath and let it out. Then he turned to Jimmy Olsen, the eager young man who had gone from copyboy to budding photojournalist in the span of one short year.

Jimmy looked up from his doodlings on a pad. "Yessir?"

"Have you seen Kent this morning?" asked Perry.

"Not me, Chief," Jimmy replied—and turned red as soon as he'd said the word. Lois sympathized with him.

After all, "Chief" was Perry's least favorite nickname. And thanks to Clark, the boss was already hot under the collar.

"I, uh, was in the photo lab all morning," Jimmy said quickly. "I didn't see anybody at all."

Perry scowled. "Well then, we'll just have to start without Clark, I guess."

Lois sighed. She knew how much Perry liked Clark, liked her, and liked the fact that the two of them had finally got it together.

Still, it seemed sometimes that the old guard newspaperman didn't like the idea of an office romance. To Perry's way of thinking, there was always the potential for a falling out between her and Clark—which could destroy a beautiful writing partnership.

"Start without *whom*?" Clark asked, as he slipped in through the conference room door.

Lois smiled. "Nice of you to join us," she remarked.

Clark shrugged good-naturedly. "Well, you were all having such a good time talking about me, it seemed a shame to interrupt."

Everyone laughed—even Perry, who

mercifully refrained from raking Clark over the coals for being late. Without another word, Clark sat down next to Lois and took out his pad.

Only when he was settled did Lois find Clark's left hand and squeeze it gently under the table. Almost immediately, her independent, strictly-business side admonished her for showing affection on the job—even when Clark was the only one who knew it.

But more and more, Lois was learning to ignore that part of her. She took a moment to steal a glance at her partner.

I wonder how I didn't see it earlier, she thought. Glasses on, glasses off, hair wavy and dry, hair slicked straight—big deal of a disguise.

Once I came to see the truth, I felt silly for not knowing all along. Clark Kent doesn't look all that different from Superman. But I guess attitude and situations can really affect how we see somebody. Nobody looks at Clark Kent expecting to see Superman, so all they see is Clark. And nobody looks at Superman expecting to see Clark—or anyone else, for that matter.

Not that seeing Clark is a bad thing, she told herself. Inwardly, she smiled. Nope, she mused, it's a pretty good thing.

"All right then," said Perry, breaking the mood. "Let's get down to the news." He was serious now, letting everyone know that it was time for work.

Jimmy patted Clark on the shoulder,

genuinely glad to see him. Lois, Clark, and Jimmy were a triple-play combination that seemed natural together. They were balanced and comfortable with one another's quirks. No one would have thought to sit between them.

"Unfortunately," Perry continued, taking a seat at the table, "there isn't much in the way of headline news. Except for this confounded heat wave, that is. And if I see one more blasted story about *that*, I'm going to burst a blood vessel."

"There's got to be *something* happening in Metropolis," Jimmy piped up. "It's a big—well, metropolis, after all."

"Sure is," Lois chimed in. She refrained from looking at Clark as she spoke. "Who knows? Maybe Superman put the brakes on some nefarious plot by Intergang this morning."

She was fishing for information as to Clark's whereabouts earlier that morning, not only out of personal curiosity, but in the genuine hope that there might actually be something newsworthy there.

"And he could just as likely have been off building a community pool," Clark replied. "Or preventing a derailment on the Ninth Avenue Subway line."

"Well," said Perry. "*That's* news." He instructed one of the other reporters to follow up on it. "I've got a few other ideas simmering. They've just yet to—"

He was interrupted by the ringing of the conference room's wall phone.

"I'll get it," Jimmy volunteered.

But Perry waved him away and got it himself.

"White here," he said. "Yes, Julie. Thanks for getting back to me." He placed his hand over the receiver for a moment. "Julie Sullivan from the Metropolis Film Commission. One of those possibilities I mentioned."

Lois looked at Clark. "I wonder what it's about," she whispered.

"Maybe the Chief is looking for a second career in show business," Jimmy offered quietly, trying to keep a straight face.

Clark held his pencil in his hand like a cigar and affected a Groucho Marx voice. "I didn't know he had a *first* career in show business."

Lois shook her head. Sometimes it wasn't hard to believe he was a visitor from another planet.

Perry continued his conversation, ignoring the repartee of his reporters. "You can, Julie? Aw, that's terrific. Sure. Uh-huh. I owe you one, Julie. Thanks again. Bye."

As Perry hung up the phone, he looked to Clark. "Seeing as you're so good at impersonations," he said, "I'm sending you and Lois undercover on a little assignment."

"An assignment?" Lois echoed.

"Uh-huh. You'll be spending the next few days on the set of *Bolt*."

"Who or what is a Bolt?" asked one of the other reporters.

Jimmy looked at her incredulously. "You really don't know?" he asked. "It's that movie they're filming in Centennial Park. I was going to try to get myself on the set this week. The movie stars Beau Paris. I'm a big Beau Paris fan."

"Beau Paris?" Clark echoed.

"Jeesh, Clark," said Perry, "don't you ever get out to the movies? Beau Paris is a big Hollywood actor. There was even talk of him playing the King in a new big-screen biography."

"The king of where?" asked Lois—even though she knew the answer.

"Now don't you go poking fun at Elvis, young lady," Perry shot back. "Anyway, *Bolt* is this big-budget, robo-Robin Hood type movie that Beau's starring in. The director—uh, what's his royal highness's name again?"

"Dorian Hatch," answered Jimmy.

"Yeah. This Hatch fellow, he agreed to shoot the movie in Centennial Park after the film commission cut a deal with him. In fact, they gave him the place for free—the idea being to drum up future film business. After all, in the old days, they used to shoot lots of films in Metropolis."

"But what was in it for Hatch?" asked a reporter from the back. "He could just as easily have shot the thing in some remote forest."

"True," Perry replied. "But apparently he

28

thought it would draw attention to the film if he shot it here. And free publicity is free publicity."

"It worked, too," Jimmy noted. "At least at first. Then all of the big entertainment news shows stopped covering the movie. I heard somewhere that it was going to fall short of expectations."

Perry nodded. "The only newsworthy angle on *Bolt* is whether or not it will be Hatch's last work for Hollywood. Seems there've been several accidents on the set in the last few weeks. And nothing trivial, I might add. We're talking major accidents—sets collapsing, that sort of thing."

"Why haven't we heard anything about this?" asked Lois, upset with herself for letting something even vaguely newsworthy go unrecorded.

"They've been covering it up," Perry explained. "Hatch has been able to convince the police and the film commission that everything is under control. But this morning a stunt double for Paris nearly got decapitated when his motorcycle malfunctioned and kicked him off like a rodeo bull."

"Stunt double?" Jimmy asked, clearly surprised. "That's strange. Paris is famous for doing his own stunts."

"Exactly, son," Perry shot back.

"Are you suggesting these weren't accidents at all?" Clark wondered.

His boss shrugged. "Doesn't it sound that way to you?"

Clark leaned back in his chair. "If Hatch's career is one bad picture away from being flushed down the tubes, perhaps he's looking to hedge his bets by sabotaging his film—and cashing in on the completion bond."

"What's a completion bond?" asked Jimmy.

"It's a sort of insurance," answered Clark. "The financial backers of a movie take out the bond against the possibility that the movie never gets finished. It's become standard operating procedure for big-budget films."

"And if Hatch has a piece of the bond," continued Lois, picking up Clark's train of thought, "then he could have his cake and eat it, too. If the movie looks like it might flop—which, apparently, it does—he could keep it from ever being finished and he would still make a hefty profit. And his reputation is protected to boot, since it was some 'mysterious sabotage' that kept *Bolt* from reaching the screen and no fault of his own."

"Now you guys are cooking!" exclaimed Perry. He eyed Lois and Clark. "All right then, here's the game plan: Julie got you two jobs on the set. Lois, you're to go undercover as Claire Sullivan, Julie's cousin. She's lined up a spot for you as a production assistant, attached directly to the film's production coordinator."

"And what about me?" Clark asked.

"You're a production assistant, too," Perry told him. "But Julie figured you'd have better

30

access to the behind-the-scenes staff and equipment if she assigned you to the special effects crew. You'll have the same boss as Lois, but you'll be working hands-on with a different group of people. That way the two of you will cover more bases. Clark'll be going undercover with the name Louis White—one of my favorite relatives."

Lois grunted. "One question, Perry. Why is this person on the film commission helping us get a scoop?"

"Good question," Perry conceded. "Let's just say Julie owes me a favor or two. Plus, if these accidents continue and one of them finally proves fatal, the commission stands to lose a lot of future business. On the other hand, if we can nail down what or who is behind the accidents, we can keep Metropolis's image clean—and get an exclusive in the bargain."

"Sounds good to me," said Lois.

"Then get going," Perry told her. "You and Clark are excused from the rest of the meeting."

"Me too?" asked Jimmy, hopefully.

The boss shook his head. "Not this time, Olsen. We want to infiltrate the crew—not outnumber it."

"We'll call for help if anything comes up," Lois told Jimmy. Then she headed for the door, with Clark close behind her.

"Allow me," said Clark, reaching past Lois to open the door for her.

"Why thank you," she said, "Clark—I mean Louis. Can I call you Lou for short?"

Her fiancé smiled. "Call me anything you want, Lois. After all, you're good with names."

It was true. It was Lois who'd first tagged Clark with the name "Superman" in a front page scoop.

As they emerged into the bustling *Daily Planet* city room, Lois found herself eager to get started—even if it meant they would soon have to leave the crisp, air-conditioned confines of the office to brave the excruciating outdoor heat.

"So . . . what's our strategy?" Clark asked.

The two had long ago got into the habit of discussing the division of labor on a story. This kept them from becoming competitive with each other—which had been a problem when they first met.

Lois shrugged. "Since you'll be near all the equipment, it'd probably work best if you checked out the props involved in each accident."

"That makes sense," Clark agreed. "And what about you? What will you be doing while I get a 'grip' on things?"

She thought for a moment. "I'm going to get close to the personalities behind the scenes. I want to know who could have done what to whom and why they would do it."

Clark nodded. "Sounds like a plan."

Lois was glad she and Clark would be doing

the undercover thing together. Early in her career, she'd been strictly the independent sort. But now she enjoyed working side by side with someone—especially when it was Clark.

After all, they were more than partners. They were two people in love with each other—one of whom just happened to be able to bend steel in his bare hands.

CHAPTER THREE

Rolling a dry twig between his hands, Colin stood at the edge of the clearing and watched the developing love scene between Beau Paris and Arlee Atkinson. As Colin looked on, Paris turned to Arlee, pulled her close to him, and kissed her on the lips.

Colin sighed. What he wouldn't give to be in Paris's shoes right now, he thought. After all, Arlee was one of the most attractive women he'd ever seen. And, being an actor, he'd seen plenty.

"Cut!" cried Hatch.

The director stalked out into the sun-drenched clearing, where Paris and Arlee stood all by themselves. "What is she?" he asked Paris. "Your sister? Your pal?"

"What the blazes are you talking about?" Paris spat back at him.

"I want to see some romance," snapped Hatch. "I want to see some *sparks*."

Paris jerked a thumb over his shoulder at the sweltering sun. "*You* swelter out here in this oven, Hatch. I can barely stand, much less make love to anyone."

"If it was easy," Hatch shot back, "anyone could do it. You're supposed to be an actor, Paris. Do some *acting*."

Paris looked as if he were going to say something more. Instead he pressed his lips together and turned to Arlee.

"Let's try it again," he snarled.

Colin turned away from the clearing and headed for the lunch trailer. But by the time he got halfway there he'd forgotten all about Arlee.

There was a brunette sitting on a picnic table outside the trailer—a brunette in red shorts and a white tank top, with long legs and a killer smile. And she was looking at him, as if she'd been watching him for some time. He swallowed hard.

"Not a gawker like the rest of this bunch?" the brunette asked him.

"Er . . . no," he stammered.

The woman swept back a lock of raven hair and extended her hand. "I'm Claire Sullivan," she said. "The new production assistant."

"Pleased to meet you," he told her. "Colin Dunn."

"I know," said Claire. "I saw you in *Seven Sisters*. You were great."

Colin was relieved. She had at least seen a film of his that wasn't too bad. He'd been in some pretty awful pictures as well—the same kind *Bolt* was shaping up to be.

"Thanks," he told her. "I don't suppose I could interest you in some pasta salad? And maybe some pleasant conversation on an incredibly hot day?"

The woman shrugged. "Why not? I'm on a break."

Colin smiled. Maybe something good would come out of this film after all.

* * *

"You know," said Lois, picking at the last of her pasta salad, "if I didn't know better, I'd say you weren't exactly thrilled to be here."

She was careful not to give herself away by being too curious. Colin could be a good source of information.

"That's putting it mildly," he told her. He looked around, obviously to make sure no one was listening to him but her. "This whole movie is a farce, y'know."

Lois's ears perked up. "Why do you say that?" she asked.

Colin hesitated. "You promise you won't tell your boss, Claire?"

"Cross my heart," Lois promised

He sighed. "This is not what Robin Hood is all about."

Lois eyed him. "You speak like a man who knows a lot about the subject."

Colin grunted. "I suppose you could say I'm sort of an expert on the source material. My grandfather, Bruce Dunn, played Robin Hood in the very first movie made about the legend. A *silent* movie, that is—but one with style. It really captured what Robin Hood meant to people."

Lois nodded sympathetically. "And *Bolt* is just a special-effects, play-to-the-lowest-common-denominator rehashing of that tale."

"You said it," he replied.

She was beginning to see a suspect as well as a potential source of information in the person of Colin Dunn. Perhaps he was sabotaging the film out of some sort of loyalty to his grandfather. Lois leaned in closer.

"Of course," Colin added, "it's still good publicity for me, what with the historical tie-in to my family, and I need to showcase my ability somewhere. Plenty of stars do their earliest work in crummy movies. Humble beginnings and all that."

So much for a prime suspect, Lois mused. It was unlikely Colin Dunn would jeopardize his own rising star in a fit of family loyalty.

"Well," she offered after a brief pause, "this is one crummy movie that may not make it to the screen after all."

He looked at her. "You're talking about all the accidents."

Lois nodded. "Except not everyone is calling them accidents."

"Maybe you're right," Colin agreed. "Maybe Hatch is so sure he has a stinker on his hands, he's hoping to junk the project and cash in on the insurance."

He wasn't really serious about that theory, at least not as far as Lois could tell. However, that was the theory Clark had expounded as well— the one about the completion bond that Hatch had taken out on the movie.

"You don't seriously think Dorian Hatch

would put people's lives in danger just to bank some cash?" she asked.

Colin smiled. "Claire, you're obviously new at this. Don't ever make the mistake of believing that Dorian Hatch has a conscience. He'd do anything to anybody to get what he wanted." He paused. "That is, with the notable exception of Arlee Atkinson. The two of them are madly in love. If Arlee wants the movie to hit the screen, Hatch will walk through a bee's nest in a honey suit to finish it for her."

"But that raises the question of whether the leading lady cares one way or the other about finishing the film," Lois pointed out.

"That's true," Colin agreed.

Food for thought, Lois told herself. But she and Clark were scheduled to rendezvous in a few minutes, and it seemed she'd pumped Colin for all he knew—at least for the time being.

"Well," she said, "I'd love to stay and chat, but duty calls."

Colin nodded. "Yeah, we all have things to do." He smiled hopefully. "See you around the set, then?"

"You can bet on it," she told him.

Rising from the table, Lois dropped her paper plate and plastic utensils in a nearby garbage bin and headed for the production trailer. It was the last one in a long line that began with the lunch trailer and included all the stars' dressing rooms.

Casting a final look over her shoulder at

Colin, she saw him wave. She waved back. Then she made her way through the trees. The production trailer was just over the next rise. Clark would be waiting for her there.

As she walked, she went over in her mind what she had learned from Colin; specifically, that Hatch was as ruthless as a viper, and that he wouldn't let anyone stand in his way. On the other hand, the director had a soft spot for Arlee Atkinson and thus might have a reason to want to finish the movie. Dorian Hatch was a definite suspect, if not a perfect one. *Yet*.

Lois wiped the sweat from her forehead and glanced at her watch. Damn. She was running late. That was bad. Neither she nor Clark wanted to be away from their jobs any longer than they had to. It would jeopardize their cover.

However, as she came in sight of the production trailer, she felt a breeze stir the otherwise dead, still air. A *familiar* breeze. In the next moment, she caught a glimpse of a red and blue blur as it flashed across the blazing afternoon sky, and she knew immediately that her plans had changed.

"So much for our rendezvous," she murmured.

Lois was annoyed, but not terribly so. After all, it wasn't the first time Clark had left her to change into Superman.

Changing direction, she opened the door to the production truck and was blasted by a welcome rush of near-frigid air. Oh well, she told herself. At least I can cool off for a minute. Thank heavens for the air conditioner.

"Claire?"

She turned and saw her boss, Mary Chase, pointing at her. The woman had a cordless phone against her ear.

"Yes?" Lois replied.

"I need you to run a few errands for me." She held up a fistful of pink memo pad notes.

"Out *there*?" asked Lois, pointing to the door through which she'd just entered.

"Out *there*," the production coordinator confirmed.

Resigning herself to the situation, Lois nodded. "Whatever you say, Miss Chase."

Wherever he was, she hoped Clark was enjoying himself more than she was.

CHAPTER FOUR

As he raced across the Metropolis skyline, Superman was filled with regret. His efforts as Louis White on the set of *Bolt* had so far revealed very little.

He still had no clue whether the string of accidents was anything more than mishap and coincidence. And now, to make matters worse, he was forced to leave Centennial Park just minutes before his intended meeting with Lois.

Of course, rescues and robberies needed his immediate attention as Superman. There was no way around that. But being Lois's reporting partner was equally important.

Fortunately she'd be able to get along all right without him. After all, Lois had been a star reporter in this town before Clark arrived on the bus from Smallville. She didn't need him to help crack a case.

Shifting his weight slightly to the left, Superman altered the path of his flight, aiming himself toward Hob's Bay. This is the second time today I've had to speed off to Suicide Slum, he thought, as the cityscape blurred beneath him.

Perhaps it was time he had a super hero-to-politician chat with the city council. Sure, they had a lot to handle, but they needed to work harder at improving conditions in this part of the city.

And particularly in the vicinity of the Hob's Bay Nursing Home. If the radio report he'd heard was correct, a power cut had blacked out four city blocks—including the one with the nursing home. In other words, there was no electrical power for air-conditioning.

Normally, that wouldn't have constituted a job for Superman. By law, all city nursing homes were equipped with back-up power. However, the back-up system had failed in this case. And to make matters worse, the news reported that the city was having some sort of problem getting emergency vehicles to the site.

Excruciating heat and a lack of power—a dangerous combination indeed, especially where the elderly were concerned. But now that he was here—

Suddenly, as Superman descended toward the block in question, his breath caught in his throat. "I don't believe this," he said aloud as he neared the ground.

When he'd heard about the power cut, he had chalked it up to the overuse of air conditioners in Metropolis. He'd never dreamed that the cause was something else. Something so silly—and so eminently preventable.

There was a gaping pit at his feet that dominated the center of the street in front of the nursing home. The hole was nearly ten feet across. It was crawling with city works employees and all sorts of equipment.

Approaching the nearest worker, he tapped the man on the shoulder. The man, who hadn't noticed him because of the noise of a pneumatic drill not far away, did a double take.

"Superman?" he exclaimed. "What are *you* doing here?"

The Man of Steel tilted his head to indicate the pit and all the laborers in it. "What's going on?" he asked.

"What do you mean?" said the worker.

Superman frowned. "What made you decide to dig a hole in this street on the hottest day ever in the history of Metropolis?"

"Oh," replied the workman, "that. Well, we were replacing the power lines in this section of the block so that this here nursing home would be safe from a blackout."

"Safe from a blackout," Superman echoed. The irony wasn't lost on him.

The worker nodded. "Yeah. But one of the lines got sliced by this here powerdrill." He pointed to a monstrous-looking piece of heavy equipment that was sitting in the middle of the pit.

"Well," said Superman, "tell me where the slice is, I'll solder it with my heat-vision."

The man grunted. "Did I say slice? It's more like *shredded*. And I don't have enough cable on-site for you to splice in a fresh stretch."

"And as soon as the line was broken, power was shut off to this section of the grid," the Man of Steel concluded.

"That's right," the worker confirmed. "It'll be

hours before the cable's replaced, and even longer before the system comes back on line."

"I get the picture." Superman sighed. "Thanks." He turned and headed for the front door of the nursing home.

"Hey, it's not my fault," the workman shouted at Superman's back. "I just lay cable."

No doubt the man was right. It wasn't *his* fault—but someone had slipped up, or the folks in the nursing home wouldn't be in this predicament.

Clark's own adoptive parents, Jonathan and Martha Kent, were getting on in years. And though they were healthy and active, and would likely never require the tender mercies of a nursing home, Clark couldn't help imagining them in a similar plight.

Putting the thought aside, he turned his attention to the task at hand. He had to evacuate the people in the building to a safer facility—and he had to do it quickly, before they succumbed to the gathering heat.

Opening the front door, he was confronted with a vision of chaos. Orderlies were rushing the home's clients to the main lobby, carrying them down several flights of stairs, in many cases. After all, Superman thought, heat rises. As hot as it was here, it was getting even hotter on the higher floors.

He turned at the squeal of rapidly approaching sneakers. A middle-aged woman with graying hair drawn back into a bun was zeroing in on him.

"Superman!" she shouted, her voice echoing in the confines of the lobby. "Thank the stars." The woman wore a dull brown trouser-suit and a white lab coat. She held out her hand. "I'm Dr. Stacey," she said. "As you can see, we have quite a situation here."

"So I see," he replied.

The doctor frowned. "Only a couple of these people can walk under their own power, and there aren't enough wheelchairs to go around. And with the mess the street is in—"

"Sorry to interrupt," said Superman, "but I've got to get started. I can take one patient at a time, maybe two if they're in good shape."

Stacey sighed. "And where will you take them? Your place?"

The Man of Steel looked at her. "You mean you haven't arranged with another facility to house them temporarily?"

"Oh, I tried," the woman replied. "But this is a state-funded institution, the only one in the city. There are several private facilities in Metropolis, but they don't open their doors to the poor."

"They do now," Superman stated flatly. "I can be pretty persuasive when I want to be. Where's the nearest facility?"

Stacey's forehead wrinkled. "The closest one with enough available space is over in Park Ridge," she decided, "the Ridgeway Hills section."

45

"Ridgeway Hills," Superman repeated. It was one of the ritziest parts of town. "Well," he said, "your patients are going from economy to first-class in a hurry, aren't they?"

"And they'll be flying Superman Airlines," Dr. Stacey observed with a faint smile.

The Man of Steel smiled back. Then, knowing each moment he delayed only increased the possibility of fatalities, he crossed the lobby and scooped up the nearest patient—a plump, white-haired woman in a pink cotton robe. She blushed as she gazed into his eyes.

"My lord," she breathed, "no one's picked me up this way in forty years. Are you sure you'll be all right, young man?"

Superman smiled. "I'll be fine, ma'am. Now just relax, and I'll take care of the rest."

Over the next two hours, he made forty-two round trips between the Hob's Bay Nursing Home and Shady Acres Rest Resort in Ridgeway Hills. At first the head administrator at Shady Acres, a Mr. Styles, wasn't too pleased about the unexpected deliveries, but the compassion of his doctors and nurses, as well as the very vocal support of the home's clientele, soon convinced Mr. Styles that he'd have a mutiny on his hands if he didn't graciously open his doors. Superman was pleased to see that even the well-to-do had room in their hearts for those who needed help.

Depositing the last patient at the door of Shady Acres, the Man of Steel watched a couple of nurses slide the man into a wheelchair. The patient waved to Superman.

"Thanks again," he called.

Superman waved back. "Don't mention it," he replied.

Then he whipped his cape behind his back and sprang into the air. In a moment, he had reached a height from which he could look down on Shady Acres—which was now the temporary home of all those who might have perished in the heat back at Hob's Bay.

Then, as he flew past the huge clock that hung suspended between the twin monoliths of Carlini Towers, Superman's thoughts suddenly turned from the heroic to the mundane.

"Oh, geez," he said aloud.

He hadn't only missed his rendezvous with Lois, he'd missed a good deal of the workday on the set. And his boss, Miss Chase, wasn't likely to look very kindly on that.

If I don't get back there soon, he thought, I'm the one who's going to need to check into Shady Acres.

Then he looped around and speared through the air toward Centennial Park.

CHAPTER FIVE

As Clark put his glasses back on and slipped through the trees to return to the production trailer, he could see that something was wrong. There were production assistants wandering all over the place, trying to grab what little shade they could. Each and every one of them looked profoundly, pitifully oppressed.

"What's happened?" he asked of no one in particular.

If anyone heard him, no one bothered to reply. In fact, everyone was so drained by the oppressive heat that they couldn't even muster up the energy to look at him.

I'd better find Lois, he thought. She'll know what's going on around here.

Walking more briskly toward the trailer, Clark noticed that its door was wide open—a clear sign in this heat that something was wrong. And there were crumpled sheets of yellow paper strewn about the base of the stairs.

What's more, now that he listened for it, he could hear Lois's voice. And she didn't sound happy. Not at all.

Poking his head in, he saw that she was sitting at a desk with her back to him. She had a phone in her hands and a Metropolis Yellow Pages— open to the section marked "air-conditioning contractors."

Lois's white tank top was matted to her back with perspiration—an indication that the air-conditioning was no longer working inside the trailer. And if Clark needed another clue, all he had to do was listen.

"No," Lois shouted into the phone, "*you* listen. I don't care if you're bidding on a contract to fix all of the air conditioners on the moon! We've got a unit down here that needs repair!"

Lois paused for a moment, listening to the voice at the other end of the phone. Clark couldn't see much of her face, but it seemed to him it was screwed up tightly. A moment later, however, her expression became remorseful.

"Oh, a nursing home," Lois said contritely. "Well then, can you recommend anyone—hello? Hello?"

Muttering something under her breath, Lois tore the offending page out of the phone book, crumpled it in a tight little ball, and threw it at the stairs. No doubt she intended for it to join the other balls of crumpled paper that had accumulated there.

Clark watched the paper bounce off his chest. Then he caught it before it could hit the ground.

"Lose something?" he asked.

It was only then that Lois realized he was standing there. She turned and stared at him blankly, apparently too exasperated and too exhausted to work up any resentment.

"Where have you been?" she asked.

Clark pointed at the phone. "Would you believe at that nursing home?" he said, trying not to smirk.

"Busy place," she replied flatly.

"Very busy," he said, looking up at Lois. "Power cut wiped out the cooling system. I had to evacuate everyone."

"You can give me the details later," she told him. "I've been given the task of finding an air conditioner repairman willing to make his way into the park to fix a single unit—and on a day when *everyone's* trying to do the same thing. So, as you can see, I'm not a happy camper."

That much was obvious, he mused.

Turning back to the phone book, Lois ran her finger down the page of listings again, looking for the next number to call. Then, suddenly, she turned to glance at him again.

"So? What did you find out before you flew out of here?"

Clark sighed. "Not much, I'm afraid. And you?"

"Well," Lois began, wiping perspiration from her forehead with the back of her hand, "before this disaster struck, I got some pretty juicy insights from one of the co-stars in the movie— Colin Dunn."

Lois related what she had learned from Dunn—about his familial connection to the project and his rather low opinion of Hatch. Clark had to admit that it was juicy, all right.

But as Lois began to wind down, something else grabbed Clark's attention. What's more, it must have been obvious, because he felt Lois's grip on his arm.

"Clark!" she rasped. "Are you listening to me?"

Unfortunately, he wasn't. Or more accurately, he couldn't. Not if he was going to concentrate on . . .

"Gunshots!" he hissed.

Lois looked at him. "What?"

He frowned. "I've got to go. There's an armed robbery in progress somewhere near the park."

With that, he turned away from Lois and began to head off into the trees. He'd already divested himself of his glasses by the time she stuck her head out after him.

"Can't you let the police handle it just this once?" Lois asked halfheartedly. But she already knew the answer to that.

Ducking behind some trees, he completed his transformation. Then he took off so quickly that an observer couldn't have tracked him—only felt the wind he created with his passage.

Lois slumped against the jamb of the trailer door and grunted. She hadn't seen Superman take off. She had only heard the rustling of the leaves.

With a sigh, she returned her attention to the phone book and the task at hand. However, before she could dial another number, Lois was disturbed once again. "Claire?" said a voice.

Turning, Lois saw that it was Mary Chase who had interrupted her. "Yes?" she replied, sweeping a wet strand of hair off her face as she did her best to fashion a smile.

"Claire, have you seen Louis White around anywhere?" Mary asked.

Lois often covered for her partner, even if he *was* proving rather useless in this case. "As a matter of fact," she said, "I *did* see him briefly."

"Great," remarked Mary.

It was obvious to Lois that the woman was at least mildly perturbed.

"No one's seen him since this morning," the production coordinator went on.

"What's wrong?" asked Lois.

"Well," said Mary, "with the air-conditioning out, my people are going through the beverages like . . . well, like water."

Mary laughed dryly at her own little joke. Lois let out a polite chuckle in response.

"I wanted to send Louis out to restock the supply," the coordinator continued, "but that man is never around when you need him."

"Isn't *that* the truth," Lois said softly, looking up at the sky.

"What?" asked her boss.

"Oh, nothing," Lois replied quickly.

"Well," said Mary, "he and I are going to have a serious talk. That is, whenever he shows up for work again."

Lois tried to think of a way to shield Clark. "Listen," she said, "I may have been overstepping my bounds . . . but I sent him to get more drinks already. That's where he is now."

Mary looked at her. "*You* sent him?"

Lois nodded. "Uh-huh." Great, she thought. Now we'll both get thrown off the set, him for never being around, and me for insubordination.

But instead of biting her head off, the coordinator smiled. "I'm glad to see you're on top of things, Claire. You know, you're good at this job. I wouldn't mind bringing you aboard the next time I need a P.A."

"Let's see if I can get these air conditioners fixed first," Lois replied.

Mary nodded. "See you later, then," she said, then ran off to tackle another production crisis. Before she'd left the trailer, she was already on her walkie-talkie.

Lois sighed. Terrific, she told herself. Just terrific.

Now she would have to get the caterers to come back to the set to deliver more drinks. But first she would take another shot at the air conditioner problem.

Lois punched the keypad on her phone. A man answered in a rough voice.

"Yeah?"

"Dreher Heating & Cooling?" she said. "I need a hero."

53

CHAPTER SIX

Ricky Pataki leaned over the service counter at the Big Belly Burger and waved his gun in the cashier's face.

"Listen," he said, "we want what we want, and you want to stay alive. So do what I tell ya and everybody'll be happy."

The cashier, a pimply-faced kid wearing the name "Elvin" on his Big Belly badge, swallowed hard. His eyes were fixed on the wisp of blue smoke wafting from the gun's barrel—the last evidence of the warning shot Ricky had fired just above Elvin's head.

"Whatever you say," said the store's manager, a not halfway bad looking blonde who had come out from the back at the sound of the gunshot. "We don't want any trouble."

Ricky smiled. We don't want any trouble. That's just what they said in the movies.

He could hear his mother's voice in his head. Get a job, Ricky. It builds character.

Ricky's mouth twitched, a nervous tic that he'd developed some time ago. Sure, he thought. Get a job and make peanuts. Or hold up the Big Belly Burger and make a bundle in a few minutes.

Keeping his gun pointed squarely in Elvin's face, Ricky shot a glance at his buddies, Freddie and Mickey. One of them stood at either entrance to the place, keeping an eye on the street and on the dozen or so customers in the restaurant who sat sweating over their Big Belly Burgers.

"Everything chill out there?" Ricky asked.

"Chill, all right," Mickey confirmed.

"Frosty as a Big Belly Freezie," added Freddie.

"A Freezie," Ricky echoed. He grinned at the thought. Sweat trickled down the back of his neck. "Now, that is a silver idea, Freddie. This heat's a killer."

Ricky pushed the gun closer to Elvin's pudgy nose.

"All right, Big Belly Boy," he laughed. "I'm ready to give you my order." Ricky used the barrel of his pistol to point up at the menu above Elvin's head.

"We'll take—" he began.

But he stopped when something flashed across the security mirror attached to the wall above the menu. Taking a step back from the counter, he pointed his weapon at a black man who had silently risen from his seat.

"Uh-uh-uh," Ricky said, with a shake of his head. "I don't know where you think you're going, but ol' Elvin here would take it mighty personal if you just ate and ran. Now sit down."

The man did as he was told.

Ricky turned back to Elvin. "As I was saying," he went on, "we'll take three extra-fat, chocolate Big Belly Freezies—to go."

Elvin stared blankly at Ricky. "Really?"

Ricky nodded. "You want anything else, fellas?" he asked over his shoulder.

"All the money in the registers," answered Mickey.

"Oh, yeah," Ricky said with a grin, "I almost forgot. We'll have a side order of cash."

"Would you like fries with that?" Elvin asked, his voice cracking.

Ricky laughed with genuine feeling. "You are funny, my man. But with this blasted heat, we don't need no hot food. I'll just take the dough and the shakes."

Elvin looked to the manager. At a nod from her, he pushed two buttons on his cash register. The drawer immediately popped open, and he began filling a red and white striped Big Belly bag with the money.

"You're doing great, friend," Ricky said.

Then he stopped aiming the gun at Elvin's chest and instead waved the barrel at the two other cashiers behind the counter. They blanched at the sudden attention.

"Take the lead from your boy here," Ricky told them. "Fill up some bags. And *you*," he said to the manager, "make with the shakes."

The cashiers nodded in fear and did as they were told. At the same time, the manager moved to the Freezie machine and began filling an extra-large cup with thick chocolate goo.

A minute later, the cashiers handed three

bulging bags full of cash to Ricky. Mickey and Freddie left their posts at the doors to help Ricky hold the money.

Suddenly the shake machine let out a terrible whine. It grated on Ricky's nerves.

"What's going on?" he snapped.

"W-we're out of ch-chocolate," the manager replied, trembling.

"Typical," Freddie said. "Make mine strawberry, then."

"Vanilla for me," said Mickey.

"I'm partial to cherry," came a voice from seemingly out of nowhere. Ricky turned around, but he couldn't seem to zero in on who had spoken.

"Who said that?" he demanded.

The assembled customers just looked back at him. No one took responsibility for the remark.

Ricky's jaw clenched. It was time to get out of here. Turning back to the manager, he was about to tell her to give them what she had made and to forget the rest.

But when he brought his eyes level again, he was no longer looking at the manager. What he saw instead was the distinctive red "S" of a certain super hero.

"Oh, geez," groaned Mickey, before the stunned Ricky could even speak.

Ricky looked into Superman's steel-blue eyes. "H-how'd you . . . ?" he stammered, trying to find his voice.

"The drive-through window," answered the Man of Steel.

Superman assessed the three would-be holdup men. They were more like kids, actually. He doubted that any of them was more than nineteen years old—even their leader, who was standing across the counter from him. But they were still armed and dangerous, and there were people in this restaurant who might get hurt if a scuffle were to follow.

"We are walking out of here," the gunman said with forced confidence.

"That's all right," the Man of Steel replied, keeping his voice light and casual. "No need to work up a sweat walking. I'll just fly you down to the local police precinct."

"No way," the boy returned. "We're leaving alone."

Then he cocked his pistol. Apparently he'd formulated some kind of plan and was confident he could make it work. This was not the time for Superman to insist otherwise.

"Bullets," Superman said, looking pointedly at the teenager's gun. "Don't you read the *Daily Planet*? I don't do bullets."

"Oh, yeah," said the boy. "I knew that." He tilted his head to indicate the restaurant's patrons. "But the rest of these flesh-and-blood saps do."

Superman smiled. "I'd make pretzels out of

those peashooters before you could pull the trigger," he said.

"Maybe," the boy conceded. "But this one is already aimed at you. And I'm betting that not even you could stop six ricochets off your chest before one of them found a home in someone else's."

The Man of Steel frowned. "Okay, then," he replied. "Take the money and leave."

The gunman hesitated. He seemed to be looking for some kind of duplicity in Superman's expression, but he wouldn't find any.

"Mickey, Freddie . . . let's move," the boy said finally.

Still eyeing Superman, he took a cautious step backward. Superman stood his ground while the three robbers moved farther away from him and closer to the door.

Then, at a speed so fast the human eye could not follow his movement, the Man of Steel launched himself over the counter. The boy couldn't have seen him move—but he had to have noticed that Superman was no longer standing where he had been.

The teenager fired the gun in the general direction that Superman had come from, but he got off only a single shot before his adversary grabbed his weapon and twisted it into more curls than a Big Belly french fry.

A heartbeat later, Superman had done the same to the other two guns. In the seconds that followed, he picked up some metal stools and wrapped their legs around the gunmen's wrists. Then he twisted the stools together, so the would-be robbers couldn't go anywhere.

Their leader looked dazed. "How'd—?" he stammered.

"You made a mistake," Superman explained. "In coming up with your ricochet theory, you forgot to compute what the change in distance between you and me would do to the bouncing bullets. I just waited until you got far enough away that I'd have time to deflect your shot up into the ceiling. Sort of like playing pool. You play pool?"

The teenager shook his head.

"Well," Superman went on, with a final twist of the iron bars, "you'll have plenty of time to learn. Two to five years, I'd think. I hear the state prison has some lovely recreation rooms."

CHAPTER SEVEN

One hour after he had left Lois poring through the Yellow Pages, Superman exited the local police precinct, determined to do his fair share of investigative reporting.

He had delivered the Big Belly gunmen to the authorities. And even though he had to wait around for a few minutes to give an official statement concerning the crime, there were plenty of hours of daylight left. Superman took to the sky, prepared to make the one-minute flight back to the set.

Unfortunately, crime refused to take a holiday in Metropolis. Twenty seconds shy of a safe, secluded landing, a fresh set of screams attracted his attention.

Superman gritted his teeth with determination, never once thinking that he could ignore the cries for help. Someone was in trouble. His duty and responsibility were clear.

Executing a tight turn, he headed for the trouble spot as quickly as he could, his cape fluttering loudly behind him.

The air in Centennial Park was still filled with tension—but Lois was beginning to get used to it.

She sat inside the production trailer talking with her boss, sipping cans of Soder Cola, enjoying the cool breeze that blew from the freshly repaired air conditioner. But all the while, Lois was keeping an eye on what was going on outside the trailer's big side window.

From her vantage point, she could see nearly everything that was happening on the set. Right now, Lois saw that the crew was setting up for the next shot, a mere thirty yards from the trailer.

"You're turning out to be quite a miracle worker, Claire." Mary raised her can of cola in a mock toast to her assistant. "Quite a miracle worker indeed."

Lois blushed with fake modesty. "It was nothing, really," she said with a small smile.

"No, not nothing," Mary insisted. "You follow instructions well, you have great suggestions, and you're not afraid to take the initiative. You're a go-getter."

"Thanks," was all Lois could think to say. She genuinely liked Mary Chase and was beginning to feel a slight twinge of guilt over the lie she was putting over on the woman.

After all, to Mary, "Claire" was a production assistant. But Lois Lane was there strictly to dig up dirt. To the reporter, Mary was nothing but a source of information.

"And speaking of go, as in always gone," the woman went on, "where *is* that Louis White? I still want to have a talk with him."

Lois's mind raced, looking for another way to cover for her always-absent partner. "Well," she began, "I'm not really sure. He said something about one of the gaffers needing a bulb. He must be off dealing with that."

Mary frowned. "Whatever. Finding a bulb shouldn't take more than a few minutes. And neither should picking up these soft drinks, really." She seemed disappointed. "I guess he's not your responsibility, Claire, but he's not the worker I was told he'd be. I'd better start seeing some results from him. If he doesn't shape up, I'll have to give him the boot."

Lois grinned nervously. "I'm sure he's just getting his feet wet. Then he'll show you something."

Mary looked at her askance. "You sound like you want to keep him around," she observed slyly. "Why, if I didn't know better, I'd think you had a crush on him, Claire." The older woman shrugged. "He *is* easy on the eyes, after all—work or no work."

Lois cleared her throat. "He is that," she admitted. "But," she hastened to add, "my interest is purely professional. I figure if I can keep a slacker like him around, it'll make the job I do look even better."

Mary laughed. "Uh-huh. Purely professional." She displayed a knowing grin. "Whatever you say, Claire."

Lois turned to look out the window for a moment, trying to avoid her boss's piercing gaze.

She hoped that her expression didn't reveal her true feelings about Clark.

Out on the set, just inside the ring of cameras, the crew was about ready to shoot. In the scene they were working on, Bolt would be sleeping on the forest floor while, unbeknownst to him, a pack of hungry wolves would surround him. Of course, the camera filters would make it look like night—more Hollywood magic.

Lois could see Paris speaking with Hatch and a man she knew to be the wolves' trainer. She couldn't hear what they were saying, but she could guess that Paris was upset about something by the way he was flailing his arms. Hatch had a hand on the trainer's shoulder, in a grip that suggested confidence.

Mary followed Lois's gaze out to the set. "This is actually one of my favorite scenes in the movie," she commented.

"Really?" Lois asked without removing her eyes from the set. "It makes me sort of nervous, what with those wolves wandering around." Apparently, it made Paris nervous too.

"Well, don't be shaky. Those wolves belong to Alan Sbarra," she said pointing at the red-haired trainer. "He's the best animal man in the business. Those puppies don't even breathe unless he gives them permission first."

Lois turned to look at Mary. She saw her opening and like the reporter she was, she took advantage of it.

"That's good to know," she began. "But with all the accidents that have happened around here lately, I wouldn't care if he had those wolves under some sort of mind control. It seems awfully risky to me to have your star surrounded by a bunch of ravening predators."

Mary chuckled. "So you don't think that everything that's gone wrong on the set is merely a bunch of unrelated accidents?" The woman took another sip of her cola, letting the question hang in the air.

That was a very reporterlike query, Lois thought. Which one of us is undercover here?

"Why?" she asked Mary. "Don't *you* think that they've been accidents?"

Her boss put down her can and shrugged. "Actually, no—I don't," she said. "I think someone in particular is behind each and every one."

Lois glanced at Mary. "Really?" she asked.

"Uh-huh." The production coordinator leaned a little closer, as if guarding against any eavesdroppers. "I've been trying to add it up," she continued, obviously looking for someone to share her theories with. It was a role that Lois was more than happy to fill.

"Do you know who I think is behind it?" Mary asked.

Lois ventured a guess. "Dorian Hatch?"

"Hatch?" The woman laughed. "That's a good one." Suddenly she stopped laughing and looked at Lois in a new light. "Why do you say Hatch?"

Lois shrugged. "It's no secret that he's got a big piece of the completion bond," she provoked, interested in the response.

"The insurance money?" Mary seemed to think about it for a moment. "No, I don't think so. Hatch isn't about money. Sure, dating Arlee Atkinson can put a vacuum-cleaner-sized drain on the old bank account—but in my opinion, too much of Hatch's reputation is tied up in this movie to see it go swirling down the tubes."

"Then who?" Lois inquired, perhaps with a bit too much enthusiasm.

Mary folded her arms triumphantly and leaned back in her chair. "Beau Paris," she said with authority.

"Paris?" Lois was a bit shocked at the certainty in her boss's voice. "But the biggest accident of all nearly broke him into little pieces. How could it be him?"

"Think about it, Claire. The motorcycle crack-up may have come close to taking Paris out of action. But in the end, it *didn't*. He was conveniently not on the bike when it went bust." She paused. "Maybe that wouldn't be such a big deal if we were talking about some other actor. But Paris is famous for doing his own stunts. And he shied away from this one."

Lois stroked her chin thoughtfully. "You know for certain that he took himself out of the scene?" she asked.

"No," said Mary, "not for certain. But the

only people with that authority are him and Hatch. And why would Hatch have taken Paris out when he's left him in so many other scenes?"

The coordinator lifted her soft drink can to her lips and took a triumphant sip. Lois watched her, the gears meshing in her mind.

"So Paris wanted to kill his stunt double?" she probed.

Lowering the can, Mary shook her head. "I don't think he had murder on his mind."

"Then what?" asked Lois.

She was anxious for her boss to fill in some of the gaps. The woman had an angle on the case, one that Lois was willing to believe was possible. But she needed some facts to pursue.

"Simple," Mary replied. "Revenge."

"Revenge?" Lois asked incredulously. "On whom? And for what?"

"On Hatch," the coordinator told her. "For Arlee Atkinson. After all, Paris and Arlee were once quite an item, until she left Paris for Hatch."

Interesting, thought Lois. Paris and Arlee had once been lovers. Unrequited love was a powerful motive to do some pretty stupid things. But Lois would need more to go on before she could file her story.

"So you're saying Paris would sink his career because his heart is broken?" Lois shook her head skeptically. "I don't think I can buy that. Women like Atkinson must be three for a nickel in Hollywood."

"True," Mary conceded. "But there's more. When I was in Hatch's offices back in Hollywood, I happened to see Paris's contract for *Bolt*. It seems his salary is guaranteed up front."

"Oh?" said Lois.

"That's right," her boss confirmed. "He's taking several million dollars to the bank instead of signing for a smaller sum and a percentage of the profits on the back end. And you know taking a piece of the pie is all the rage these days. Why would Paris forgo a profit clause unless he knew he wasn't going to finish the film?"

"That's a good question," Lois agreed.

Paris certainly had a motive. Plus, he had ample opportunity to set up the accidents. In her mind, Paris moved into a close second to Hatch in the suspect race.

"And," Mary went on, "here's the clincher. A friend at the Kerschner Casting Agency told me Paris has a handshake deal to star in a huge romantic thriller—if he can be available by the end of this month for principal photography. Now that's three whole weeks before *Bolt* is scheduled to finish." She raised an eyebrow. "See what I mean?"

Lois nodded. I think we have a new leader, she decided silently.

"What about Colin Dunn?" she asked. She had already decided that he wasn't a suspect, but it wouldn't hurt to hear Mary's assessment of the man.

"What about him?" the coordinator responded. "He's an adequate actor and a good-looking guy, but I don't see your point."

"Do you think he could be involved in these accidents?"

Mary shrugged. "Why him? His family connection to the legend of Robin Hood? That's the very thing that landed him this role. We figured it would generate a human interest angle for the publicity people—though that doesn't seem to have happened."

"Yes," Lois added, "but maybe he's the one who's jealous. Jealous of Paris's stardom and angry at Hatch's hatchet job."

"I doubt it," her boss said. She looked past Lois at the action on the set. "He's a good guy. And he knows he's a picture or two away from lead actor status. It would be foolish for him to—"

Mary stopped dead in midsentence. At first she just looked puzzled. Then her eyes filled with terror.

"Oh my God!" she shouted, leaping to her feet.

Lois turned to follow the woman's gaze. What she saw made her want to cry out, too.

It was the wolves—the trained animals who were supposed to gather around the sleeping Bolt. They'd gone berserk!

CHAPTER EIGHT

Both women raced for the door. Lois, being a little younger and a little quicker, got there first. Once outside in the oppressive heat, she could hear the screams of the cast and crew. However, two other noises clearly rose over their shouts— the stern, booming voice of Alan Sbarra and the feral growls of his supposedly well-trained wolves.

"What's happening?" Lois asked, gripping the arm of a husky gaffer.

"They're out of control," the man told her. "Get out of here, unless you want them to take a piece out of you!"

Despite his advice, Lois approached the set, her reporter's instincts taking over. And her boss wasn't far behind.

By then, nearly everyone had cleared out of the way. Hatch and the animal trainer, however, stood just inside the ring of cameras. And Paris lay on the ground, a wolf no more than six feet away from his throat while the others circled around the actor like vultures.

Paris put his hand out in a stop sign. "Nice doggie," he said with a quiver.

The wolves just growled. The one nearest to him growled the loudest of all.

"Don't move," Sbarra shouted, both to the wolves and to Paris. "Misha!" he said. "Heel!"

The wolf nearest Paris ignored Sbarra and instead took three steps closer to the leading man. Paris shook so hard he looked as if he'd been caught in an earthquake. The wolf licked saliva from its lips and bared a row of sharp, glistening fangs.

"Do not move, Mr. Paris," commanded the trainer. "Do not speak. And most of all, do not let her smell your fear."

"Don't speak?" Hatch hissed indignantly. "Are you nuts? This could be our best scene." He tilted his head toward the only cameraman still left at his post, the one who sat atop a tall moving crane. "Keep that camera rolling, Phil. Paris, deliver your lines. Do it *now*."

The actor glared at Hatch with venom in his eyes. He began to say something but halted himself when Sbarra raised a finger to his lips.

"Quiet," he mouthed.

Then he turned to the wolves again. He seemed to summon up all the forcefulness in his lean, spare body. "Fang, Percival, Misha—sit!" he demanded.

That's when the wolves seemed to forget about Paris and instead threw themselves at their master. Sbarra went down in a heap of muscled, lethal grey fur, his scream for help cut short by the wolves' fury.

Suddenly, before anyone could utter another word, a blue and red figure streaked into the fray. Pulling the wolves away from the animal

71

trainer's throat, the figure interposed itself between Sbarra and the snarling beasts.

Lois breathed a sigh of relief. It was Superman, returning from his latest emergency. For the first time that day, she was glad to see that Clark wasn't on the job.

With blinding speed, the wolves hurled themselves at the newcomer, one after the other. Their jaws closed on his arms, on his legs, round his throat—but all to no avail. He wasn't called the Man of Steel for nothing.

Before the animals could hurt anyone, Superman tucked one of them under his arm and grabbed the other two by the scruffs of their necks. And in a dramatic flurry of red cape, he took off into the blue sky.

As Lois watched him depart, she wondered what he would do with the beasts. Probably deposit them at the Metropolis Zoo, considering it was the closest facility available. The wolves could be subdued there and cared for. And examined, of course, to find out why they had turned on Paris and Sbarra.

"Man," said Hatch, shading his eyes to see Superman's exit. "What I wouldn't give for someone like *him* to be working for me."

He already does, Lois mused.

"What a man," said Mary, as Superman disappeared.

Lois nodded. "Yup." But her mind was no

longer on her boyfriend. "I wonder what set those wolves off on a rampage?"

"I can't imagine," the coordinator replied.

"Maybe they were drugged," Lois ventured.

"Or maybe they didn't like Beau's aftershave," Mary quipped, her voice trembling a little.

It seemed to Lois that the woman was having a delayed reaction to the horror of what had happened and was using humor to try to calm herself. Whatever works, she thought.

"My babies," moaned Sbarra, whose skin was mottled and scratched from his brush with death. And yet he didn't seem to care a bit for himself— only for his wolves. "What will happen to them?"

"Who cares?" muttered Hatch. "We're insured."

Paris stormed up to him and poked his finger into the director's chest. The actor's face was a bright, angry crimson.

"You're crazy, nuts, certifiable! You would have let those wolves kill me!" he railed. "You would have let them tear me to bits!"

"I would've got some genuine emotion, for a change," Hatch insisted, brushing Paris's finger away. "If that's the only way to get it . . ."

The actor's eyes blazed. "Why," he snarled, "I oughtta tear you apart—"

Before he could put his words into action, Arlee Atkinson interposed herself between the two men.

"Now, boys," she said, "do we really need all this shouting and chest thumping?" She put her arm around Hatch's waist. "After all, what did Dorian really do? He simply took advantage of a bad situation to make you look even more like a star."

Paris's nostrils flared. "But he—"

"What was he supposed to do?" asked the actress, keeping her voice calm and steady. "Wrestle the wolves for you? He's an *artist*, Beau. He took a bad canvas and tried to paint a better picture."

Paris stared blankly at his leading lady. For a moment he seemed at a loss for words—almost as if she were making sense to him.

"What's going on?" asked someone behind Lois.

Realizing whose voice it was, she turned. There was Clark, standing there in his work clothes, grinning like a kid. Obviously he was pleased with himself for taking care of the wolves and zipping back in no time flat.

Lois looked at him. "Oh," she said, "it's you."

"Sorry I missed all the excitement," he told her, leaning closer to Lois so he could whisper in her ear. "At least I got here when it mattered."

Lois put a hand on Clark's chest and pushed him away from the group into the surrounding trees. What Lois had to say wasn't at all for public consumption.

"You got here in time to keep that animal

trainer from getting gored," she pointed out. "But that's about *all* you've done around here."

Clark looked at her helplessly. "Lois, that's not fair. I—"

"Not fair?" she echoed, not giving him a chance to finish his statement. "How's this for not fair? While you're off doing who knows what, I'm stuck here doing *both* our jobs—not only as reporters but as production assistants as well. And all the while, I have to keep coming up with excuses as to why 'Louis White' is never around."

Clark sighed. "Are you finished?"

"I'm finished," she confirmed.

He frowned—something she didn't often see him do. It showed her that he wasn't too thrilled about the way things had turned out, either.

"All right, then," he said. "I'm sorry you've had to bear the burden of this investigation on your own, and I'm sorry you have to keep covering for me.' But this has been one especially disaster-filled day. Maybe it's the heat, I don't know, but it seems like *everyone* needs Superman today."

"That's just my point," Lois told him. "Why do people need a super hero to handle every little problem for them? There are police, community service organizations, paramedics— all sorts of normal agencies set up to handle emergency situations."

Even as she said it, she knew she wasn't

speaking rationally. It was her frustration talking—her resentment at having to shoulder the burden of their work on the set alone. And maybe the heat was getting to her, too.

But all the same, she couldn't stop herself. The words were coming out, and there was no way to take them back.

"But I just can't ignore it when people cry out for help, you know that," Clark maintained. There was hurt in his voice, and disappointment as well. Being Superman wasn't just a lark for him, she knew. It was a calling.

Lois felt her heart go out to him. It softened her anger.

"No . . . I guess you can't," she sadly conceded, putting her hand on Clark's arm. "But one time, you're going to respond to some distant cry for help . . . and miss another cry, closer to home."

He knew just what she meant. She could see it in his eyes.

"What am I supposed to do?" Clark asked.

She thought for a moment, but there was no easy answer.

"I don't know," Lois responded. "I just don't know."

She turned away from him. It was too hot for an emotional conversation like this one. But then, these things never seemed to come at convenient times.

"I guess it comes down to a matter of

priorities," she went on. "I know, for myself, when I'm faced with having to do one important thing and a second or third important thing suddenly pops up, I plow ahead with the first one while keeping the other emergencies at bay. Otherwise, I'm liable to end up with three raging fires instead of three manageable ones. At least that's the theory."

"It's a tough thing to do," Clark said. "And it's even tougher when people's lives are at stake."

She turned back to him. "I know that. But lives are also at stake on this set. Just ask that animal trainer. Ask Beau Paris. And if we don't solve this soon, I'm afraid this whole movie will be shut down—in which case the bad guy will get just what he wants. Or worse yet, somebody'll end up dead."

Clark bit his lip. He knew she had a point.

"I want to be able to count on you, Clark," Lois told him, "and I'm beginning to think that I can't."

Suddenly, before Clark had a chance to reply, something caught Lois's eye, distracting her. She looked past him and saw that Mary Chase was heading in their direction.

Clark began to speak. "Lois, I—"

Abruptly he stopped, even before Lois could make a move to hush him. Superhearing, she thought. It comes in handy, doesn't it?

"Mary," she said, turning her attention to the

approaching production coordinator.

Mary smiled. "There you are, Claire. And you, too, Louis. Apparently there's at least one thing on this set that commands your attention." She looked pointedly at Lois.

The reporter laughed. "Oh, no," she tried to explain. "This isn't what you think. I, ah, I was just . . . "

"Claire was just reading me the riot act," Clark explained. "She's worried that I'll make our friend at the film commission look bad."

For once, Lois thought, he's making an excuse for me. That's refreshing.

"Yeah, that's it," she added. "You caught me, Mary."

Their boss arched an eyebrow at Clark. "Well, mister, that's not the only riot act you're going to hear today." She turned to Lois for a moment. "We're going to finish for the day, so you can head home."

Lois hesitated, glancing at Clark. "Oh. Okay," she said finally.

"I'll walk out with you," Clark offered.

Lois wasn't sure she wanted Clark's company right then. They obviously hadn't finished discussing their problem, but she was too tired and angry to hear Clark repeat his "Superman belongs to everybody" speech.

She couldn't help agreeing with the sentiment, of course, but sometimes the implications of Clark's being Superman were overwhelming. Luckily for Lois, Mary took the decision out of her hands.

"Oh, no you don't, Louis," the woman said sternly. "You and I are going to have a long talk about your work habits. Then we're going to review your responsibilities here on the set. And then—"

Lois walked away from the wincing Clark and the suddenly fiery production coordinator. A part of her sympathized with him, of course.

But Lois was only human. And a part of her was glad to see him squirm for leaving her in the lurch at Hollywood East.

CHAPTER NINE

An hour later, Lois dragged her sweat-soaked body through the front door of her apartment. She had contemplated stopping by the *Daily Planet* on her way home, but there was really nothing to be done there.

And after her argument with Clark, she just didn't feel like being around people. Unfortunately, as Lois pushed the door closed behind her, she knew she wasn't alone.

"Clark?" she called out tentatively.

She peered across the living room. A shadow was moving across the refrigerator in her small, cloistered kitchen. It *could* be Clark, she thought. Mary could have railed at him for fifty-nine minutes, and he still could have beaten her here.

Crossing the living room, she poked her head into the kitchen. Lois sincerely hoped it wasn't a burglar. She was too tired to have to deal with something like that.

As it turned out, it wasn't a burglar at all. It was her sister Lucy, with a plastic container full of tuna salad in her hand.

"No," said Lucy. "It's only me." She smiled that patented Lane smile. "Sorry to disappoint you, Sis."

"I'm not disappointed," Lois told her. "Believe me."

Heading back out into the living room, Lois

Perry White (Lane Smith), Jimmy Olsen (Justin Whalin), Lois Lane (Teri Hatcher),
Clark Kent (Dean Cain), Martha Kent (K Callan) and Jonathan Kent (Eddie Jones)

Lois Lane and Clark Kent

Superman

Lois Lane and Superman

Lois and Superman

Jimmy Olsen

Lois Lane

Clark Kent and Lois Lane

dropped her purse on the couch and flopped down next to it. She should have continued the conversation, but she just couldn't find the strength. All she could do was lie there and soak up the welcome iciness of the air-conditioning.

"Don't get up," said Lucy, joining her on the couch with the container of tuna in her lap. She plunked a tall glass of iced water on a side table and picked at her dinner with a fork. "I wouldn't want you to work up a sweat or anything, y'know?" She looked at Lois and grimaced. "Oops, too late."

Lois sighed. "Sorry I'm not more presentable," she said sarcastically, tilting her head to look up at her younger sibling. "How are you doing?"

Lucy shrugged. "Fine, I guess. Just came by to steal some dinner on my way to work." She chuckled. "You, on the other hand, look like something even the proverbial cat wouldn't drag in. Tough day?"

"The toughest," Lois told her.

She eyed the tall glass of iced water that her sister had brought in. A drop of water made its tantalizing way down the side of the glass.

"Oh, here," said Lucy, "have some water." She handed Lois the glass.

Lois found the energy to nod. "Thanks."

Accepting the glass, she propped herself on one elbow and drank so fast she dribbled water down her chin.

"So," Lois said when she came up for a gulp of air, "what brings you here?"

Lucy pointed at the container of tuna. "Free food," she replied. "Remember?"

Lois felt ridiculous. "Oh yeah. I guess you said that already."

Her guest looked at her with some concern. "Lois," Lucy began, drawing her sister's name out so that the syllables sounded like two distinctly separate words, "come on, it's *me*. Your sister. Don't play ditzy. I can tell there's more bothering you than just hot and nasty Mr. Sunshine." Her eyes narrowed. "Now give. What's up?"

Lois just let her head fall back against the sofa and closed her eyes.

"What is it?" Lucy badgered. "Work? Clark? Bad hair day?"

"All of the above," Lois responded.

"So give me the details," her sister pressed.

Lois remained silent.

"Come on," Lucy cajoled. "It'll make you feel better. Free venting of frustration. Two ears, no waiting."

Lois tilted her head to look at her sister. At first she was going to make some excuse not to talk, to just keep her feelings to herself, but Lucy's face was so inviting in her eagerness to listen, to help. The gates opened, and Lois purged herself of her anxiety.

"It's like this," she started, "Clark and I are

working together on a story. Well, we're *supposed* to be working together."

Unfortunately, Lois couldn't say anything about Clark being Superman. She shared a lot of secrets with Lucy, but that wasn't one of them.

"Anyway," she continued, "he hasn't been much help."

Her sister looked at her. "Clark? The Boy Scout in reporter's clothing? Has he been sick or something?"

Lois paused to think of a way to frame her response. She couldn't tell Lucy the whole truth, but maybe an abridged version would suffice.

"You could say he's been sick," Lois responded. "Not cough and sneeze sick, but . . . well, let's just say he's off his game. Distracted."

Lucy's brow furrowed. "You two aren't having problems, are you?"

Lois shook her head. "No, not like that. He just isn't into the partner-on-a-story thing right now. He's not putting in the effort."

"Listen to you," her sister said. She mushed the tuna around with her fork. "You sound like a whiny wife."

Lois took offense at that. "I do not!"

"Do too," Lucy insisted. "'Clark isn't pulling his weight,'" she mimicked. "So what? There was a Lois Lane, Wonder Reporter, long before there was a Clark Kent, Associate Wonder Reporter."

True, thought Lois.

"Is he treating you poorly?" asked Lucy,

knowing the answer in advance. "Is he trying to take advantage of your work habits? Backsliding? If he is, ditch the bum."

Lois looked at her sister, stunned by that last bit.

"Or," Lucy went on before her sister could speak, "is there something else on his mind—something that has nothing to do with you or your work? A family problem, maybe?"

Not exactly, Lois thought. But she couldn't stop her sister from speculating—not without revealing the truth about Clark.

"You know," Lucy continued, "Clark never struck me as the type to wear his heart on his sleeve. Maybe he's going through something that's keeping his mind other places. You guys have a good thing going, but it might take him a little while before he confides everything in you."

Lucy let her words sink in, giving her sister time to pick from column A or column B. Was Clark a louse or a mouse? Lois knew he was neither. She also knew there probably wasn't much Clark wouldn't confide in her.

"Lois," Lucy persisted, perhaps afraid that she hadn't quite nailed down her point yet, "Clark's a great guy. Better than anyone *I'm* ever likely to meet. But there are bound to be rough patches in *any* relationship. How you two smooth it out is what's important."

Lois stared at her sister for a second, surprised

by her level of insight. Lucy's not a kid anymore, she thought. She had actually made sense.

"You're right, I guess." Lois sighed. "And one way or the other, we *will* smooth it out." At least I hope so, she added silently.

She put her hand on Lucy's knee and swiveled to an upright position. Then she pushed herself up from the couch.

"I'll have to wait and see what choices Clark makes," Lois decided. "But no matter what, Lois Lane is going to crack this case. On her own, if need be, just like any other self-respecting Wonder Reporter."

Lucy grinned. "Attagirl, Big Sister!"

"Tell you what," Lois said, heading for the bathroom. "I'm going to take a shower . . . "

"A cold one, I hope," Lucy laughed.

Lois cast a look back over her shoulder. "In this heat? Ice cold. Will you still be around when I'm done?"

"Uh-huh," her sister assured her. "I'll be right here."

"Good," said Lois. "You can watch *me* eat *my* dinner."

She entered the bathroom and closed the door behind her, leaving Lucy to her tuna fish. Suddenly, she had an urge to add something. Opening the door a crack, she called, "Lucy?"

Her sister glanced back at her. "Yes?"

"Thanks," said Lois.

Lucy smiled. "I'm just pointing out the

obvious," she remarked. "Just pointing out the obvious."

Clark sighed. Louis White was undeniably in hot water.

"I'm sorry," he said sheepishly. "It won't happen again. I'll work twice as hard tomorrow."

"*Three* times as hard," Mary Chase said angrily. She looked at her watch. "Well, I have better places to be, so you're off the hook for now. Just don't let it happen again."

"I won't," Clark assured her.

The production coordinator had spent the better part of the last hour reviewing "Louis White's" performance to date as a hired hand on the set of *Bolt*. And after her tirade was over, she had made Clark lay out his duties for the following day, so he wouldn't be able to use miscommunication as an excuse for not meeting his responsibilities.

Leaving Clark behind, Mary joined the stream of crew members leaving the park for their hotel rooms. Only a security staff would remain on hand overnight to watch the props and equipment.

Clark contemplated his boss's words. He could still feel their sting. Boy, he mused, compared to Mary Chase, Perry's a walkover.

Making sure to take a different direction from Mary, so he wouldn't accidentally bump into her again, Clark headed for home on foot. After all that he had done that day, it would feel good to not have to fly.

He hadn't got very far before someone cornered him, though. Despite the gathering shadows, he recognized the man as one of the actors.

"Uh, Mr. White, is it?" asked Dunn, putting his hand out to Clark. "Colin Dunn."

"Yes, of course," Clark replied. He shook Dunn's hand. "What can I do for you, Mr. Dunn?"

"You can call me Colin, first off. Mr. Dunn was my father."

Clark laughed politely. "All right. Colin, then. And you can call me Cl—" He coughed to cover his mistake. "Er, Louis."

It was hard enough keeping *one* secret identity straight. *Two* was almost impossible.

"Good," said Dunn. "Louis it is." Colin paused and clasped his hands together nervously. "Louis, I was wondering, uh, if you could fill me in about that other new production assistant. You know, Claire Sullivan?"

"Fill you in?" Clark replied, a little surprised.

He had heard that sound in a man's voice before, that particular lilt that gives away a person's intentions when he or she is smitten with someone. In this case, it seemed, Dunn was smitten with Lois.

Not that Clark could blame him. He knew the feeling only too well.

"Yeah," Dunn responded, a little embarrassed. "Her background, likes and dislikes, whether she's seeing anyone. That sort of thing."

"Oh," Clark mocked gently, "a professional question."

Dunn laughed. "Well, you know . . . " He left his words hanging, waiting for Clark to provide some answers.

The reporter eyed him. "What makes you think *I'd* know those things?"

"Well," said Dunn, "I saw the two of you talking together before, sort of heart-to-heart. I figured you were friends." He laid extra emphasis on the last word, probing for information.

"Friends," Clark echoed, finding he preferred to be vague about the subject. "You could say that."

He fought down an instinct to be territorial. He didn't want to give away anything about his personal life that might tip off his true identity as a reporter.

"*Just* friends?" Dunn pressed.

"*Good* friends," Clark emphasized, raising his eyebrows.

"But not dating?" the actor persisted.

Boy, he won't give up, Clark thought. "Not dating *tonight*," Clark offered politely.

Dunn was momentarily puzzled by that last answer. Clark used the actor's hesitation to escape.

"Anyway," he said, "Mr. Dunn . . . Colin . . .

it's been a very long, very hot day, and I need to be here early tomorrow." Still facing the other man, Clark took a few steps back. "I really need to get going."

Dunn began to ask another question, but Clark, who was a master at extricating himself from one place to race off to another, pretended to be out of earshot.

"Good night," he called. And a moment later, he managed to slip away through the trees.

It really *had* been a long day. The sooner Clark put it behind him, the better.

Colin Dunn watched the dark-haired production assistant vanish into the gathering gloom. For a moment he just stood there, pondering what he had learned from the man.

"Not dating tonight," Colin repeated softly.

He began to walk toward the park's southern exit—in the opposite direction from everyone else, since he wanted some time to himself. On his right, the sinking sun seemed to be setting the trees ablaze with its fiery light, but he barely noticed it. He had other things on his mind.

"Does that mean she's available?" he muttered.

Maybe Louis had hit on her and she put him off. In that event, Colin himself might have a chance with her.

He continued to contemplate the matter as he reached the street. Instinctively, he raised his hand to hail a taxi—then put it down when he spotted one across the street in front of the Centennial Park Hotel.

The actor began to weave his way across the busy thoroughfare, which was clogged with slow-moving traffic. Taxis weren't easy to get this time of the evening. He had lucked out.

Or had he? "What the—?" he said out loud.

Across the street, two people were coming out of the hotel—a man and a woman, arm in arm—and they were heading for the same taxi. What's more, they were a good deal closer to it than he was.

Colin contained his disappointment. So much for getting a cab right off the bat, he thought.

He was about to go back to the park side of the street and look for another cab when he realized what he had seen. Turning again to the couple, who were now getting into the taxi, he shook his head in amazement.

Once they were inside, the woman gave the man a passionate kiss. Then the man gave the cabdriver some directions, and away they went.

Colin stood in the middle of the street, stunned. So stunned, in fact, that he barely noticed the honking of horns, the squealing of tyres, and the curses that drivers hurled his way. After all, he *was* standing in the middle of the street.

"Beyond wild," he said softly.

But then again, he noted silently, nothing should surprise me anymore. Hollywood is Hollywood, even when it's in Metropolis.

CHAPTER TEN

Clark arrived early the next day on the set of *Bolt*, hoping to get a look at the motorcycle that had malfunctioned, nearly killing the stunt-man. Unfortunately, while he was saving lives and thwarting hold-up men the day before, the motorcycle had been packaged and shipped to the studio warehouse in California.

Or so the grips informed him before they moved on to their other chores. Clark grunted.

"So much for showing initiative," he said aloud. He put his hands in the pockets of his blue jeans, contemplating his next move.

Well, he thought, the trail has gone cold. What now, Sherlock? Of the two of them, Lois always was the better detective.

Luck, however, was not completely against him. As he stood wondering what to do next, he spied Dorian Hatch having a heated discussion with Kyle Clanton, the film's portly producer, and Mary Chase. The three of them stood near the director's office trailer, obviously not happy with each other.

"Now that looks promising," murmured Clark. He focused his superhearing to zero in on the conversation.

"Schedule, schmedule," Hatch said defiantly. "I'm the director and I'm calling for a change. Live with it."

"Look, Dorian," Clanton replied, with a hint of anger in his voice, "you can't just throw the schedule out. We're supposed to film the ending *today*. You know, the scene that requires a hundred or so extras, a fireworks display, and a ride in a hot-air balloon? What in Cecil B. DeMille's name am I supposed to do with all those people? And all that equipment?"

"Send them home," Hatch replied archly.

He punched the shooting script to emphasize how strongly he felt about this. "We need to switch gears and shoot the big disaster scene," the director explained. "The police are starting to get twitchy about the constant string of misfortunes we've had here, and the film commission is grumbling about closing us down for an inspection. Now, that'll sure put a kabosh on your precious schedule, won't it?"

Mary nodded, conceding that the director had a point. "Yes, Dorian, but—"

"But," continued Hatch, a bit more under control, "if we can get the disaster scene on film before we get shut down, we can rewrite the finale and shoot it at the studio if we have to."

Clanton was about to give the director another piece of his mind when Mary pulled him aside and spoke to him soothingly. In the meantime, Hatch watched them, ready to go at the producer again if he had to. A moment later, Clanton returned to the same spot, clearly a good deal calmer than before.

"Okay," he conceded, blowing out his tension in a long breath. "I see your point. But we're not ready to shoot the disaster scene. The script calls for Bolt's village to be torched to the ground by the Dragons, and the village isn't fully constructed yet."

"Oh, but it is," Hatch offered with a wry grin.

"What do you mean?" asked Clanton, his eyes narrowing.

The director shrugged. "I anticipated your objections so I called in a crew last night to work on the set. Another hour or so and we'll be ready to torch it."

Hatch folded his arms smugly across his chest. It was a gesture that said, Go ahead and argue with me some more. I dare you.

"Great," Clanton responded. He shook his head, as much in disbelief as in anger. "Just great. All that overtime just crushed what little leeway we had left in the budget."

He looked at Mary. She just shrugged. Obviously she hadn't known about the director's end run, either.

"Look at it this way," Hatch said reasonably. "In for a penny, in for a pound."

"Much more than a penny," Clanton replied. He chewed his thumbnail as he tried to come to grips with the changes in the situation. "Okay," he decided finally. "You've left me little choice. Go get your actors ready. And believe me, Dorian—this had better be worth it."

With that, he whirled and marched away. Though she reported to Clanton, Mary didn't follow him. Instead, she headed for the production trailer.

That's where she ran into Clark. Seeing her coming, he pretended to be on his way somewhere.

"Louis!" she called.

Clark turned and smiled, as if noticing her for the first time. "Mary. Hi."

"I'm glad you're here," she told him. "I see you took our little talk yesterday seriously."

"Absolutely," he assured her. "I—"

"There's a big change in the filming schedule," she said, cutting him off, "and I need you and Claire to get dirty."

"Excuse me?" Clark replied, not exactly sure what she meant.

"You know," said Mary. "As in roll up your sleeves." For emphasis, she rolled up her own. "The Bolt village set has to be completed in an hour. I want you and Claire to check in with the set design people and see if you can help them in any way. Doughnuts, coffee, iced water, dancing girls—whatever it takes. Understand?"

Clark nodded, amused. "Got it," he assured her.

"So get going," she told him. "I'll send Claire over when she shows up."

As Mary turned on her heel to take care of something else, Clark headed off toward the village set. Finally, he thought with a smile, I have something to contribute.

It wasn't much, but it was *something*. And for a change, *he* was looking for *Lois* now.

Halfway to the village set, Clark spotted Lois. She was on her way to the production trailer, wearing a pair of faded jean shorts and a T-shirt, ready to toil the day away under the blazing sun.

To Clark, she was a vision no matter what she was wearing. The mere sight of her made him grin.

"Lo—," he began to call out. Then he remembered that they were working undercover. "Claire! Claire Sullivan!"

Lois glanced in his direction. "Yes, Louis," she replied coolly, barely breaking stride.

He caught up with her. "You look great," he said.

"Do I?" she responded in a noncommittal way.

If she was pleased to see him, she didn't particularly show it. On the other hand, she wasn't particularly perturbed, either. In fact, she seemed rather neutral about his being there.

Clark was taken aback by Lois's lack of emotion. "Lois," he said quietly, as he walked beside her, "is something wrong?"

She dismissed the notion with a glance. "Wrong? What would be wrong?"

"You just seem a little—I don't know—distant," he said.

Ascending the steps that led up to the trailer, Lois opened the door and walked inside, letting the door swing shut in Clark's face.

Undaunted, he followed her into the refreshing confines of the air-conditioned office. They were the only ones inside.

"Not distant," Lois replied. "Just resolved."

"Resolved?" Clark was a bit bewildered. "Resolved to do what?"

"To do my job," she stated flatly. Then, with emphasis, she added, "No matter what the circumstances."

He forced a smile. "Oh, I see. This is a Superman issue."

Lois shook her head. "No issue. No issue at all."

She opened a drawer in the desk, took out the petty cash record, and looked busy. But Clark knew this was some kind of demonstration for his benefit.

"Well," he said, leaning over her shoulder, "for your information, I've been here since just before sunrise trying to dig up some clues."

He paused, hoping Lois would offer her approval. Instead, she bent over the petty cash papers.

"Anyway," Clark continued when he realized Lois would not respond, "I came across something interesting."

Lois looked up at Clark. However, she remained silent.

Clark swallowed. He didn't like this attitude—or rather, this lack of one. It was even worse than hearing Lois lash out at him in anger.

"So?" she asked at last, as if to throw him a bone.

"So," he said, "I overheard Hatch and Kyle Clanton—you know, the producer—and Mary Chase discussing a major change in the shooting schedule."

"Really," Lois responded.

There was at least a spark of interest there—a glimmer of emotion. Clark was pleased to see it. Maybe he could build on this to bridge the gap between them.

"Hatch pressed Clanton to film the village fire scene today, instead of the ending, as they had planned."

"The village fire scene?" Lois echoed, her eyes glazing over as her mind went to work on this new tidbit.

"Uh-huh. Instead of doing a day of happy ending stuff, he wants to blow things up."

She eyed him. "Did Hatch say why he wanted to make the switch?"

"He did," answered Clark. "He said he's afraid that the accidents will cause the production to be shut down. And he knows it'll be too expensive to find another location to film the village scene, now that the set's already been constructed. But the finale can be rewritten and shot at the studio."

Lois nodded. "Interesting," she said. She tapped her chin with a pencil, deep in thought. "That's great. It shows—"

Clark desperately wanted to hear the end of her thought and to tell her about Mary Chase's instructions. But suddenly, something else impinged on his consciousness.

Brake squeals. And *crashes*.

Lois knew that look on Clark's face. As he broke for the door, he muttered some kind of apology. Then he was gone, the door slamming behind him.

There he goes, Lois thought with a bit of melancholy, off to do his sidewalk act. It seemed Clark was always somewhere else, even when he was alone with her.

His superhearing was always primed for the inevitable scream for help, the sound of gunshots or explosions. Could he ever focus all his attention on one single thing? On *her*, for instance? Or would she always have to share him with the world?

Lois felt herself getting sad and angry all at once. "I am not going to do this," she said out loud. She gritted her teeth, holding back an onslaught of emotion. "I am not going to let Superman distract me from what I need to do."

Lois stood up and moved to the trailer

window. Outside, she could see workmen heading into the forest, toward the spot where the village was being completed for the movie's climactic scene. She could hear the distant whir of machinery, the ring of saw blades on metal.

I think Hatch is almost ready to be scratched as a suspect, she remarked inwardly. Almost, but not yet.

After all, he was working awfully hard to get *Bolt* into some usable form. Maybe he was just covering his tracks, making it seem that he was commited to completing this project before sinking the movie for good.

But if the day's filming went off without a hitch, any junior director could polish off the movie and put it in the can, even if Hatch walked away from the whole shebang. And that would keep Hatch from collecting on the completion bond—if there was one.

Keeping an eye on Hatch remained a necessity, just to make sure his schedule change wasn't a charade. Still, Lois was all but convinced that she should be looking elsewhere for a suspect.

Sighing, she turned from the window, grabbed a yellow legal pad and pen, and headed out into the hot summer air. She walked through the woods along a by now well-traveled path, in the direction of the village set.

On her way to the site, she passed Hatch, Beau Paris, Arlee Atkinson, and a handful of other actors. Hatch was running through last-minute instructions regarding the fire scene, in anticipation of the set's completion.

Lois took a long look at Beau Paris as she walked by. The actor stood next to Arlee Atkinson, and every now and then his eyes would flit in her direction.

Now Paris, Lois thought, is still in the running. But his stock was slipping, too. Jealousy was a powerful motive, but was it powerful enough to almost kill an innocent stuntman?

Maybe, she reflected. However, Paris had been in mortal danger himself when the wolves went out of control. She wondered what the people at the zoo had found out about the animals' strange behavior.

In any case, Paris had another reason to want to end the filming. There was that other movie offer hanging out there. But again, if today went off without any trouble, he might be able to finish *Bolt* and still have time to start the other film.

Lois looked at the group of actors one more time before she went on. Something was missing here, she told herself. Something she just couldn't put her finger on.

After a while, she broke through the line of trees and into the clearing where Bolt's village was being constructed. Metal girders and wooden planks hung everywhere, suspended from trees and built into platforms. Carpenters hurriedly put the finishing touches on the huts that made up the bulk of the title character's living quarters.

Spotting Mary on the far side of the clearing, Lois made her way through the construction crews to touch base with her. And all the while, she continued to ponder the various suspects.

I'm just not seeing something, she thought with a scrunch of her forehead. The puzzle's not complete.

Lois looked up at the village's town hall, a wood-and-thatch hut suspended fifty feet in the air on a wooden platform between two huge trees. She just hoped she could put the pieces together before they came crashing down around her.

CHAPTER ELEVEN

The Man of Steel's choice was clear—pour on the speed. Streaking through the sky toward Metropolis's St. Martin's Bridge, Superman focused all his energy on flying as fast as he possibly could.

On the bridge, the situation was dire. It was still too early in the morning to be considered rush hour, but there were enough drivers making the commute between Park Ridge and St. Martin's Island to turn what was quickly unfolding into a potential disaster.

Superman used his telescopic vision to assess the situation. St. Martin's Bridge was a one-level, six-lane metal monster, constructed in an era before safety standards were as strict as they were today.

Coming eastbound, obviously heading in the wrong direction, was an eighteen-wheel juggernaut filled with a load of metal girders. The lorry had just smashed through the token metal divider in the central reservation, and now it was skidding and swerving through the oncoming traffic.

The drivers heading into Park Ridge were in a panic. Each one drove his car off to the side as far as it could go, trying to avoid the onrushing lorry and the other cars pinballing about the roadway.

There had been seven individual crashes so

far, none of them causing any serious injuries. As far as Superman was concerned, it was a miracle that things hadn't gone worse.

Aiming himself at the out-of-control lorry, he was determined to stop it as quickly as he could. He knifed through the upper air with only that one purpose in mind.

Before the Man of Steel could close the gap, however, the lorry's loaded trailer swiveled to the left, perpendicular to the oncoming traffic, while the lorry's cab remained pointed toward an onrushing car.

To Superman, it looked like this was one head-on collision he could not stop. But he had beaten the odds before. Somehow, he would find a way to beat the odds again.

Fate and physics lent the hero a helping hand. The enormous weight of the loaded trailer caused the lorry's momentum to shift, sending it toward the outer guardrail, away from the impending smash-up. Unfortunately, the rail was too weak to hold.

With a shriek of twisting metal, the entire lorry began to tumble toward the dark green bay below. Fighting his own momentum, Superman changed direction abruptly to go after it.

As the lorry plummeted, time seemed to slow down for the Man of Steel. He could see every moment of its fall in hyper-realistic detail—the seagulls squawking, trying to get out of the way. The silent, slumped driver at the lorry's steering wheel. The spinning of the vehicle's tyres, though there was no road surface for them to spin against.

Superman's lips drew back over his teeth with the magnitude of his effort. He hurtled toward the water at top speed, reaching out as far as he could.

Just as the tail of the trailer touched the water, Superman caught up to the cab and grabbed it. Muscles straining, he changed tack again and shot upward against the mighty pull of gravity.

The bolt that connected the lorry cab to the trailer creaked miserably, threatening to break. But somehow it held. And slowly, gradually, the Man of Steel rose through the air, dragging the juggernaut behind him by its occupied cab. Before long, he was level with the road surface.

As delicately as he could, he placed the lorry on the bridge, in what looked for all the world like a war zone. Smashed and dented cars lay strewn all about, surrounded by their frazzled drivers.

Rushing around to the door of the cab, Superman tore it off its hinges. Inside, the driver lay slumped against the wheel, blood trickling from a wound on his forehead.

Superman leaned the man back in the seat. The driver was large, at least four stone overweight, and drenched with sweat.

The Man of Steel used two fingers to check for a pulse in the man's neck. Faint, he thought, the blood barely flowing. Probably heat stroke. There was no time to waste.

Pulling the man out of his seat, Superman cradled him in his arms like a baby. Then, without a word to the gathering crowd, he took to the morning sky.

How many more disasters is this blasted heat going to cause? he wondered. Veering off to the east, he headed for the closest hospital, Park Ridge Mercy General. The weather was one foe he couldn't beat, and he was spending too much time aiding its victims.

Lois was in Centennial Park, trying her best to help contain an explosion. She was standing with the film commission's safety inspector, Mick McMichael, going over the details of the upcoming fire scene.

"I assure you, Mr. McMichael—"

"Call me Mick," the inspector told her. "Now, Ms. Sullivan—"

"Lois," she corrected, strictly out of habit.

McMichael looked at her. "Excuse me?"

Lois felt herself turning red. "I mean Claire," she said, smiling nervously. She was distracted, of course, or she wouldn't have made a mistake like that—distracted not only by the story she was pursuing, but by her partner's protracted absence.

McMichael smiled back at the undercover reporter, then pointed to the safety forms she'd handed him at Mary's request. "As I was saying, Claire, your explosives crew seems to have rigged the fire charges under that village hall of yours with a forward-facing blast arc. The fire will shoot outward, into the village construct, away from the park's trees."

Lois nodded. "Yes," she told him, "that's my understanding as well. The fire will go outward." She used her arms to visually accentuate her explanation. "Outward," she said again, for emphasis.

"Well, Claire," he went on, "I'd feel better if rear-mounted blast shields were placed on each set of charges. That would ensure that the explosions go where everyone wants them to. When the shields are installed, I'll reinspect everything. Until then, I'll just need to get your signature on a couple of forms verifying the changes I requested, and then you folks can get down to making things even safer."

McMichael held out a short stack of papers and a pen. Lois eyed the forms with trepidation. After all, she couldn't very well sign off on anything official under a pseudonym, could she? Nor could she take responsibility for something so important.

Fortunately, out of the corner of her eye, she saw a familiar figure approaching.

"Claire, there you are," Mary called out, approaching Lois and the safety inspector.

Lois exhaled in relief. "Mary Chase. That's

my boss," she explained to McMichael. "She's the one who needs to sign off this stuff."

McMichael turned to the production coordinator and held out the forms. He explained who he was and what he needed.

The production coordinator nodded. "Okay," she told Lois, "I'll handle this, Claire. You check in with Hatch and see if he needs any last-minute things before the shoot."

Lois nodded. "Gotcha."

She headed away from the village center, toward the production trailers, where she figured she'd find the director. But she had barely come in sight of the trailers before she heard yet another argument between Hatch and his leading man. By now she had come to recognize their voices.

Looking around, she made sure that nobody was watching her. Confident that she was alone, she crept quietly up to the trailer and crouched beneath the window.

"Listen," came Hatch's voice, loud and arrogant. "You keep telling me you're a pro, Paris, not some acting school wanna-be. A scene's a scene. You signed up to do it, and do it you will."

"When I signed up," the actor shot back, "it wasn't nearly this dangerous. Now you've got me swinging on vines and outracing explosions."

"So?" Hatch pressed.

"*So?*" Paris blurted angrily. "So I'm not ready to do the stunts. For stuff like that, I have to

108

prepare myself, physically and mentally. Yesterday, you told me we were filming the ending. Now you tell me we're burning the village down."

"I hate to say it," offered a third voice, "but he's got a point, Dorian."

Lois recognized it as Arlee Atkinson's. She never seemed to be very far away from a Hatch-Paris sparring match.

"From what I understand," the actress went on, "our friend Beau was up late last night. At least that was the rumor."

"Great," Hatch replied sarcastically. "So big deal, he'll pull a little muscle maybe. I do that getting out of bed."

"It's possible I *will* pull a muscle," Paris responded. "Or worse. And," he added with more intensity, "if I go down, the movie doesn't get finished. Right?"

There was silence for a few moments. Obviously the remark had had the desired effect.

Was it a threat? Lois wondered. Hatch was pretty clearly fighting to complete this movie, but Paris seemed uncommitted. On the other hand, he might only be trying to save himself an injury, as he claimed. Certainly he had been placed in some real danger in the course of the filming, and a fire scene was rife with deadly prospects.

"Maybe we can use a stunt double today," Arlee offered, breaking the silence.

"Nope," said Hatch, "won't work. We only

have this set for one take and then boom—it's toast. I don't trust a stunt double to get Paris's part right."

A legitimate concern? Lois wondered. Or just an excuse to bump Paris off?

Maybe Paris, and not the completion bond, had been Hatch's target all along. But what about the accidents that didn't involve the actor? Were they just smoke screens?

Again, there was silence inside the trailer.

"Here's the deal," Hatch said at last. "You back out on me now, we get the lawyers involved. And I promise, I won't hesitate to publicize the fact that rough-and-tumble Beau Paris was too chicken to do his own stunts. On the other hand, you work with me here, help me get this scene shot, and I'll try to get you out of here early—so you can do that other picture you've been sitting on. The choice is yours."

Lois could almost feel the heat of Paris's anger. But in the end, he agreed.

"All right," he said. "I'll do it. But if I get hurt, you'll wish you'd never seen a camera. You hear me, Hatch? No accidents this time, okay?"

Hatch didn't reply. At least, not so Lois could hear him.

The reporter felt the trailer list to one side and heard the door creak on its hinges. She pressed herself against the side just in time to see Paris exit and storm down the stairs. When she was certain that he hadn't spotted her, she turned to listen at the window once again.

"It'll be all right," said Arlee. "Relax, okay?"

"I wish I could," returned Hatch.

"C'mere," the actress told him. "Let me massage the tension out of those shoulders."

There were a few seconds of quiet.

"Mmmm," Hatch finally moaned. "That makes it all better."

Again, silence. Figuring she had heard all she was likely to find valuable, Lois turned to scoot away from the trailer, still in a crouching position. But before she had taken a single step, she found herself nose-to-belly button with someone she didn't recognize from that angle.

"Um, I dropped something," she stammered, not even looking up to see who had caught her. Dropping to one knee, she ran her hands along the ground as if she were searching for something.

"No need to pretend, Claire."

Lois looked up . . .

CHAPTER TWELVE

. . . into Colin Dunn's smiling face. He reached down to her, offering Lois some gentlemanly assistance. Accepting his hand, she let him help her to her feet.

"Colin, hi," Lois said softly. She smiled, hoping to put him off guard and keep him from asking any questions.

It didn't work.

"Eavesdropping, were you?" he asked with a grin.

Lois smiled nervously. "Oh, I wasn't—" she began.

"No need to explain," he interrupted, taking her off the hook. "It's an irresistible hobby when you're around such characters as Hatch, Paris, and Arlee Atkinson."

Lois nodded. "You can say that again."

"In fact," Colin continued in a stage whisper, "I must confess to heading in this direction to do the same thing."

Lois looked at him quizzically.

"Yup," Colin replied to her silent question. "I saw something last night that shocked the hair right off the back of my neck. A little romantic rendezvous I just couldn't resist trying to follow up on."

The actor let that little tidbit hang in the air between them. Lois resisted the urge to press him, her reporter's instinct telling her that informants usually say more if they're allowed to talk at their own pace.

"Interested?" Colin asked, ready to burst. Lois's gut feeling had been right. She raised her eyebrows again but said nothing.

"Okay, you dragged it out of me," Colin said with a single laugh.

He paused a moment, apparently for dramatic effect. No doubt he hoped to pique Lois's anticipation even more.

"Well?" she blurted at last.

Colin smiled. "Well, last night when I was leaving the park . . ." he began.

Unfortunately his story was cut short by the howl of someone else's voice.

"Claire! Claire, where are you?" Mary Chase shouted.

Lois bit her lip. She was dying to hear Colin's story, and her boss was about to prevent that. Acting impulsively, she slipped her arm through Colin's and twirled him about.

"Claire!" he said.

Lois pulled him toward the end of Hatch's trailer. "Follow me," she whispered.

"What's up?" Colin asked, in the same kind of whisper. "Why are you avoiding your boss?"

"I'm not avoiding her," she told him. "Not really."

Lois swung Colin around the end of the trailer, putting the vehicle between them and the direction Mary had called out from. As luck would have it, this moved them both out of sight just as Hatch and Arlee exited the trailer and walked off in the direction of the village set.

"Why, Claire," Colin said smugly, "I didn't know you cared."

She looked at him. "I don't," she began. "I mean, I do. I mean—" She sighed. "I've just got to hear what you were going to tell me. It sounded so exciting."

"It is," Colin assured her. He leaned a bit closer, so close that Lois could smell his aftershave. "Last night," he continued, "I saw Arlee Atkinson necking like a teenager in the back of a cab."

Lois shrugged. "So?"

"So," he said smiling in a conspiratorial way, "it wasn't Dorian Hatch she was necking with."

Lois felt the pull of something important. "Arlee's cheating on Hatch? But with whom?"

Colin looked left and right, checking to make sure nobody was within earshot. "Beau Paris." He announced triumphantly. "And all the while, Hatch was probably snoozing in his hotel room."

Lois's mind went into a higher gear, examining the implications of Colin's discovery. Were Paris and Arlee together again? Did Hatch suspect?

If he did, it would strengthen his motive to want to crash the picture and fizzle out Arlee's career. However, he hadn't given any indication that he knew what was going on—at least as far as Lois could tell.

"Quite a surprise, huh?"

Colin asked the question as if he were looking for a reward. His companion, however, didn't give him the response he was hoping for.

"Yes, a surprise," she said quickly. Then she added, "Look, you'd better get going."

He seemed surprised. "Huh?"

"Mary's looking for me," Lois explained, "and I don't want her to catch us together. She might jump to the same sort of Hollywood conclusion that you did with Paris and Arlee."

Colin stared at Lois. He seemed a bit hurt. Realizing how brusque she had been, the reporter smiled softly.

"What I mean is, we wouldn't want to jeopardize my job by starting any rumors."

Colin's face lit up again. "Gotcha," he said. Then he backed away slowly and, with a wink, turned and walked away.

"Claire Sullivan!" came Mary's voice once again.

The production coordinator must have gone to her trailer looking for her assistant, then resumed her outdoor search when she discovered the office empty.

"That woman is harder to find today than Louis White," Mary muttered. "Do they alternate lazy days?"

Not lazy, Lois thought to herself as she

pressed flat against the side of the trailer, waiting for her boss to pass. Just doing other work. *Daily Planet* kind of work.

After Mary had gone away again, Lois skulked out from behind the trailer. She desperately wanted to keep an eye on Atkinson, Hatch, and Paris, and she was afraid that the coordinator might send her on some errand that would take her away from the set.

Certain that she wasn't being watched, Lois headed toward Bolt's village. She could hear the sounds of last-minute construction as she made her way through the woods.

In some ways, she thought, the suspect situation was more confused than ever. She reviewed the possibilities in her mind.

Hatch still had money as his motive. As before, he stood to rake it in if the film went belly-up and he cashed in the completion bond—an increasingly tempting prospect, no doubt, given that the filming looked more and more as if it would be a disappointment at the box office.

And if Hatch knew about Paris and Atkinson stepping out behind his back, he'd definitely have a reason to want to hurt his leading man.

But Hatch seemed to be fighting tooth and nail to complete the movie. And if he was enraged about his girlfriend's affair, he sure didn't show it. If anything, he seemed to be wrapped around Arlee's little finger.

Paris, for his part, was fading as a suspect. In

the beginning, he could have been accused of wanting revenge. But if he had Arlee back, that motive seemed a lot thinner. And the possibility of doing another, more lucrative film didn't seem appealing enough to kill for.

Besides, the wolf incident had put Paris himself in deadly danger. That made it seem unlikely that he was behind it.

However, in her new suspect, Arlee Atkinson, Lois had a number of questions worth pursuing. Arlee almost certainly knew about the completion bond. If Hatch cashed in on that, Arlee would be sitting next to him on top of a pile of money.

But in that case, why go back to her old boyfriend? If Hatch found out about it, wouldn't Arlee lose out on all that dough?

No, Lois decided, she still didn't have that last piece of the puzzle—the one that would make sense out of everything. Ideally, if she had some help at this juncture, she would be able to keep tabs on all three of her main suspects.

But with Clark off saving Metropolis, that wasn't an option. Since she knew the least about Arlee, she decided to keep tabs on the film's leading lady and hope for the best.

Lois frowned, remembering her conversation with her sister Lucy. One way or the other, she assured herself, she *would* crack this case—the same way she did it before there was a Clark Kent in her life.

CHAPTER THIRTEEN

After leaving the hospital where he had deposited the heatstricken lorry driver, Superman headed back to the St. Martin's Bridge to lend a hand.

When he arrived, he saw that city emergency crews had not yet responded to the scene—a fact that worried him. However, before he could search out the cause of that strange situation, he knew he first had to attend to the one at hand.

Landing among those whose cars had swerved to avoid the lorry, he made sure that no one was badly hurt. As he had observed earlier, there was nothing more serious than a few cuts and bruises. When the emergency crews *did* arrive, they could certainly take care of them.

Of more concern were the vehicles themselves, several of which were in no condition to move under their own power. As for the bridge, there was no real structural damage—just a broken divider and a guardrail that needed replacing.

"Hey, Superman!" called one of the motorists, dabbing his forehead with a handkerchief.

The man was standing by his white station wagon. Its front end had been crushed when it ran into a guardrail to avoid the lorry. The Man of Steel turned to him, thinking at first that the man was calling for help.

But that wasn't the case, he saw at a glance. The man was holding up his wallet, which was flipped open to display a police badge. He was an off-duty cop, and he was listening to the car radio, its volume turned up loud.

"What is it?" asked Superman, wafting across the width of the bridge to reach the man.

"If I were you," the cop advised, "I'd get down to Massequot. That's where the real trouble is."

"The real trouble?" Superman echoed.

"That's right," said the cop. "The traffic jam to end all traffic jams. If you can clear that up, we'll get some help around here."

The Man of Steel nodded and took to the air again, cleaving the hot, stale breeze. After just a few seconds of flying, he saw what the cop was talking about.

Below him, just about a mile from the bridge, was the biggest traffic snarl he had ever seen. Cars were everywhere. The three lanes of traffic heading toward the bridge held more than five lanes' worth of cars, as a horde of frazzled motorists tried to jockey for position. Even motorcyclists were unable to inch their way between the cars.

Nor was it difficult to pinpoint the cause. On any given day in Metropolis, a few cars were likely to overheat, making the roads more difficult to negotiate. But on a scalding-hot morning like this one, there were likely to be more than a few.

119

And *this* was the result. To make matters worse, the road in the direction of the bridge squeezed between two tall hills, leaving little room for any sort of shoulder or emergency lane.

Superman sighed. "City planning at its best."

As he hovered above the quagmire, he couldn't resist comparing the image to that of an enormous steel and fiberglass puzzle. Scanning further down the highway, the Man of Steel spied what he had hoped to find.

Like a speeding bullet, he shot further east and came to a sudden halt above two ambulances, a paramedical response vehicle and two motorcycle police officers. The officers were trying to calm some very disgruntled motorists, while the paramedics and ambulance attendants sat in their respective vehicles with long, tortured looks on their faces.

Superman landed in front of the paramedics.

"No time for small talk, sir," he said to the driver. The emergency response vehicle looked like an oversize minivan painted white, orange, and red. "Just hold on tight."

Bending down, Superman curled his fingers under the front bumper and lifted. Then, in one smooth motion, he gripped the front axle, hoisted the vehicle above his head, and took off into the sky.

A minute later he deposited the paramedics on the bridge in the midst of the folks who'd had to avoid the runaway lorry. The off-duty cop seemed to have taken charge by then, directing people to push the smashed cars to the side of the road where they wouldn't be so much in the way.

Without hesitation, Superman streaked back toward the traffic jam. A few seconds later, he landed next to one of the ambulances.

"You're next," he stated unceremoniously. He lifted the ambulance and flew it as fast as he dared to the accident site. Then back to Massequot, where he picked up the second ambulance. Then back to the bridge, where he let it down beside the other one.

Finally he sped back to the jam, where the two police officers' valiant attempts at crowd control were beginning to fail. Under the enormous strain of the heat, several impatient motorists had left their cars to argue with the officers.

Superman set his jaw. Things looked as if they were about to get ugly.

"Look," said one of the officers, a rookie by the look of him. He pointed to a big, burly motorist with a thick, dark beard and a cut-off denim jacket. "Just get back in your truck, buckle up, and wait for the road to clear."

The man didn't move. "Don't give me orders, boy," the driver spat. The man outweighed the rookie by at least three stone and towered six inches over him.

The cop's partner, a veteran who was greying at the temples, came up beside his co-worker. "Need a hand here?" he asked.

"Nope," the rookie responded. "But if this fella doesn't return to his vehicle immediately, he's going to wish that Superman had left one of those ambulances behind." He stared at the truck driver, making his conviction clear.

After a heartbeat or two, the driver's courage broke. With a curse, the man turned away from the two cops and rumbled back toward his idling pickup, several car lengths down the road.

After the man had lumbered away, Superman landed. The officers whirled, obviously glad to see him.

"Good job," he told the rookie, "But you and your partner should head back to the rear of the jam, before the hills, and direct traffic away from here. I'll move whatever cars I can right off the road. Between us, we'll get things cleared out here."

"Then let's get to it!" the veteran ordered.

The two cops straddled their motorcycles and slowly wove their way to the rear of the traffic jam, two miles down the road.

Most of the motorists had remained in their cars, some with the air-conditioning and motors running, others with the windows down. A good number, more than a dozen, however, were out of their cars, milling about and complaining.

Superman rose a good fifty feet off the ground.

"Listen up!" he shouted.

His voice boomed with such authority that

everyone stopped what they were doing and gave him their attention.

"I need you all to get back in your cars and fasten your seat belts," he continued. "If your engine is running, shut it off. I'm going to lift each one of you out of this mess, one at a time. Don't make any special requests as to destination, either. I'm just clearing you out so the emergency vehicles can get through."

At first the crowd didn't seem to grasp the simple orders that the Man of Steel had laid out for them. Then, slowly, those who were out of their vehicles returned to them and strapped in.

Superman leaped to the front of the mess and lifted the first car above his head.

"Ready?" he asked the two passengers.

With his X-ray vision he could see them nod nervously. Superman prepared to take off into the sky.

"Hey!" came a shout from several cars back. The huge man who had tried to intimidate the police officer leaned his head out of his truck window. "Why do they get to go first?"

"Because they're—" began Superman.

However, another commuter began to speak at the same time, this one much closer to the belligerent truck driver.

"Pipe down, buster," said the lean, lanky driver of an old beat-up sedan. He had not yet got into his vehicle. "You're keeping the man from doing his job."

"Make me pipe down!" shot back the aggressor. He opened the door of his truck and began to get out.

"Hey!" shouted Superman, trying to defuse what he knew was fast becoming the kind of confrontation he had predicted.

The two men ignored him. Their faces reddened as they hurled insults at each other.

"Enough!" Superman yelled once more. He began to lower the car he had lifted.

Suddenly, without warning, the two men grabbed each other and began to tussle. The truck driver, being right next to his pickup, reached into the front seat.

Dodging a punch that was aimed for his head, he came out swinging a monkey wrench, intent on caving in his adversary's skull.

Fortunately, Superman was as fast as his reputation. He stopped the swinging weapon just centimeters away from its intended target.

"I don't have time for this," he shouted at both men. "You"—he pointed at the driver of the sedan—"get in your car, now."

Biting his lip, the man shuffled away as quickly as he could and seated himself inside his vehicle.

"And *you*," Superman said to the trucker, putting his index finger on the man's chest and shoving him gently backward. The man landed on the seat of his pickup. "You're lucky I can't waste the effort to haul you off to the police."

Superman spun the man's legs forward, putting him in a sitting position behind the steering wheel. Then he took one end of the monkey wrench and twisted it around the man's wrists, just tightly enough to hold his arms together.

Finally he took the other end of the wrench and threaded it through the steering wheel, bending it so that it hooked around the wheel and locked into place.

"By the way, you're last," Superman said as he walked away.

The man began to say something, to make some sort of complaint, but a backward glance from the Man of Steel kept the words stuck in his throat.

Superman walked back to the car he had been forced to put down and lifted it once again.

"Clearing a path, take two," he commented out loud.

Superman flew up into the air and headed off toward the nearest service station to deposit the first of over three dozen vehicles in new locations. The task would end up taking him at least another twenty minutes.

"I sure hope that Lois can do without me a little longer," he said to a passing seagull. "It's been just one disaster after another today."

CHAPTER FOURTEEN

In Centennial Park, the heat was rising. It was still an hour before high noon, and already the sun was towering above the trees, baking everything to a crisp with its indiscriminate rays.

To make matters worse, a stale, mocking breeze had begun to blow, not strong enough to bring any real relief. The wind just threw more hot air in everybody's face.

Lois, however, couldn't let the weather, and the gallons of sticky perspiration it inspired, keep her from trailing her target. Like a mouse to Lois's cat, Arlee Atkinson could run, but she couldn't hide. Of course the reporter was careful to remain a discreet distance from her prey, waiting for just the right moment to pounce.

As Lois looked on, Arlee headed into the heart of the park's forest-like grove of maple trees, toward the area where Bolt's village had been constructed.

The set was sparsely populated right now, with most of the workers off on their lunch break. And Hatch couldn't start rolling the cameras, even though they had all been set up, because the angle of the sun made the lighting all wrong for filming.

Production would have to wait at least seventy-five minutes before the sun shifted to a better position. In the meanwhile, cast and crew had moved out of the blistering heat of the grove and into the inviting confines of the air-conditioned trailers.

Lois followed twenty yards behind the actress, wondering what she might be up to. Of course, it could be nothing, but one never knew.

When Arlee reached the village hall mock-up, she paused to look up at the trees to which the wood-and-thatch buildings were attached. Then the actress rubbed the palms of both hands against her jeans. Certain that they were dry, she grabbed one of the thick metal support beams and hoisted herself off the ground with surprising ease and grace.

Hiding behind the thick trunk of an old maple tree, Lois grunted softly. Where had Arlee learned to climb with such fluidity and athleticism?

As she looked on, the actress shinnied up the pole. When she was approximately seven feet off the ground, she stopped climbing.

Arlee tightened her legs around the pole and used her left arm to brace herself in position. Then, with her right hand, she reached out to the pack of explosive charges that dangled from the underside of the village hall's floor.

Lois had been there when the charges were first put into place. She had also been there when the safety inspector noted the projected blast angle of the explosion and insisted that a special metal blast shield be placed there—to ensure that the force of the explosion would be projected away from the surrounding trees.

Now Lois watched as Arlee Atkinson not only removed the blast shield—but turned the charges so that their pyrotechnic conflagration would be directed at the maple trees that surrounded the set.

She's booby-trapping the village, Lois thought. Arlee's the one behind all these accidents. I've got to stop her. Otherwise someone is going to get burned for sure.

But should I try to stop her here and now, Lois wondered—before she can rig any more charges? Or should I just go to the authorities and blow the whistle on her, which might give her a chance to escape?

The reporter was certain, for once, that direct confrontation was not the best course of action. She could turn Arlee in, and then the charges could be reset. What's more, the actress probably wouldn't run after fixing the explosions—she couldn't have known that she was being watched.

As the reporter bore witness to Arlee's crime, spellbound, the actress swung herself over to another pole and began adjusting a second set of charges. Lois's hesitation, however, proved her undoing.

For just as she turned to head back to the production trailer, she felt something hit the base of her skull. Hard.

Before she could react, her knees gave out, and darkness swallowed her.

Sometime later, Lois began to come to. Slowly, disoriented, she reached out from the entrapping darkness toward the blinding light of day.

Sweat streamed down her face. The back of her head throbbed mercilessly. The heat seemed to have multiplied fivefold, to the point where it stung her skin.

Get up! an impulse screamed inside her brain. Get up or you're dead!

Lois tried to sit up, but the sudden violent shift of her head and body made her queasy. She braced her hands against the ground for leverage—but even that action racked her with an intense, burning pain.

"Yowch!" she moaned, suddenly sitting up.

She was still foggy from the blow to her head, and her other senses were giving her readings that she would rather have ignored. Fighting back the darkness, she forced her eyes open— and was greeted with a vision from the depths of hell.

Lois craned her neck to look in every direction. All around her, Bolt's village and the surrounding park was engulfed in flames. The sky itself was barely visible past the thick, black plumes of smoke rising from one structure after another.

She found herself sitting directly underneath

129

the village hall mock-up, where earlier—how much earlier she didn't know—she had spied Arlee Atkinson carrying out her act of sabotage. The mock-up was a ball of flame, barely recognizable except for a vague, skeletal outline.

Sometime between Lois's being knocked unconscious and the heat-seared present, Atkinson had made good her attempt to destroy the movie once and for all.

Despite the sizzling heat, Lois was frozen with fear. Her eyes darted all about her, looking for an escape route through the conflagration. Her terror increased when she realized that there was none.

"Superman," she attempted to scream, but the word came out in a raspy cough, her lungs full of blistering smoke.

She wanted desperately to know that he was on his way to rescue her, as he had done countless times before, but she knew it was not so. Clark had left the park hours before on another of his missions of mercy, and if he *had* returned to the movie set, it certainly wouldn't be on fire now.

Lois attempted to get to her feet, but she was still weak. She crouched on her knees, tears streaming down her cheeks—tears caused by the roiling smoke that engulfed the entire area.

She listened for the sounds of relief, for the sort of noises a firefighting crew might make. She heard nothing but the snap and hiss of burning trees.

Then, as if in warning, came the strained creaking of timbers above her head. Looking up, Lois saw the floor of the village hall bow in the center, directly above her.

Suddenly filled with adrenaline, Lois hurled herself to the side—just as the thatch-and-wood construction came raining down from the sky. The flaming mass landed a few feet away.

The terror that forced her to move was still energizing her. Lois clenched her fists. She was fully awake and mobile now, and her senses were sharp again.

The fiery collapse of the village hall did Lois another favor. As it crashed to earth, the weight of the hall pulled down several of the metal support poles that had held it aloft, clearing what looked to be a path out of the circle of fire.

Lois turned from the center of the conflagration and began to run. After thirty seconds, her legs had carried her out of the village square, toward the part of the set that served as the villagers' living quarters.

Behind Lois, the flames began to advance. In front of her was a large clearing surrounded by several wooden huts, some at ground level, others hoisted into the trees.

These huts had not yet been touched by the fire, but the area was beginning to fill with smoke from the approaching flames. To the left, the trees were on fire at the point where they touched the clearing. To the right, the fire line was still several yards off.

As the smoke and flames swirled in their deadly dance, Lois caught a glimpse of three figures across the way. Two were standing, a man and a woman, while a third lay crumpled on the ground.

The miasma was too thick to make out just who was there. Carefully, Lois began to move toward the hazy figures. She tried to call out to them, but once more her voice gagged in her throat.

After a few steps, the smoke dissipated for a moment, giving Lois a better look. She stopped dead in her tracks—though oddly enough, she wasn't completely surprised by what she saw.

It was Arlee Atkinson and her on-again boyfriend, Beau Paris. The two stood there, engaged in what appeared to be an argument . . . over the body of Dorian Hatch!

The vision in front of Lois could have been a scene from the movie if the flames were not so real and uncontrolled. Arlee wore the same clothes that her character had worn during her rescue from the Dragons. Likewise, Paris was dressed as Bolt, complete with the character's billowing knee-length red cape.

Whether Hatch was unconscious or dead, Lois could not tell. But it was pretty clear he had come to harm at the hands of the duplicitous lovers.

Suddenly, as if in a nightmare, Paris turned

and locked eyes with Lois. Grabbing Arlee's arm, he pointed in the reporter's direction.

Lois couldn't hear their exchange of words, but it didn't really matter. Clearly, she had been spotted.

Arlee shook off Paris's hand and turned away from him. She began to run from the clearing, away from Lois, toward the part of the set that served as the village's outer wall and watchtowers.

Paris glanced once more at Hatch's body, hesitating. Then he took off at a run after his leading lady, his cape fluttering behind him.

Lois prepared herself to run also. The flames behind her were advancing steadily, leaving only two possible escape routes—one leading away and to the right, the other leading in the same direction in which Paris and Atkinson had just fled, straight past the body of Dorian Hatch.

The smoke began to gather once more, engulfing Lois. She was effectively blind now, and she knew the safest route would be to the right, away from Hatch.

But was he dead or alive? She couldn't be sure. She strained to peer through the smoke, to glimpse some sign of the director's condition.

Suddenly Lois felt the touch of a hand on her shoulder.

CHAPTER FIFTEEN

Lois turned and sighed with relief, certain that her hero had finally come—just in the nick of time, like he always did. However, it wasn't the hero she had expected.

It was Colin Dunn.

Sweat streaming down his soot-blackened face, he actually smiled. His teeth glistened in the firelight. For all her fear and anxiety, Lois couldn't help being reminded of the man's swashbuckling forebear.

"Claire? Claire!" he blurted with a cough. "Thank goodness I found you!"

"Colin?" Lois nearly choked on the actor's name. Trying to gather some oxygen into her lungs, she spoke once more. "What are you . . . ?"

"No time," he told her. "They told me you'd come this way, so I went looking for you." His chest shook with a violent series of coughs and wheezes. "The fire is out of control. People are lost—Hatch, Arlee. We need to go back!"

"No!" Lois croaked.

Not understanding her meaning, Colin grabbed her arm brusquely. "We can go the way I came," he shouted. The roar of the approaching fire made it difficult for them to hear each other speak. "Please, Claire!"

"We can't," Lois shouted back. "It's . . . it's Hatch. He's . . . " She coughed again, unable to complete her sentence. "Just follow me!"

Lois jerked away from Colin, breaking free of his grasp. Then she grabbed his hand and led him toward the spot where she had last seen Hatch. Or anyway, where she *thought* she had seen him. Right now, the smoke was too thick to see much of anything.

"What are you doing?" Colin asked.

Then the smoke drifted and swirled once more, and the actor could see why Lois had dragged him here. Hatch was still lying on the ground, unconscious—or worse.

"Paris and Arlee left him there for dead," the reporter explained.

Colin looked at her, aghast, as he began to comprehend what that meant. "Is he—?" Colin asked. "Dead, I mean?"

"I don't know," she gasped. "But we can't leave without getting him first."

Colin nodded tentatively. Clearly he wasn't looking forward to dragging Hatch out with them.

It would slow them down—and they couldn't afford to be slowed down now. But as Lois had said, they had little choice in the matter.

"Okay," he said. "You—"

But his remark was drowned out by a loud, cracking sound, like the lash of thunder over their heads. A moment later, amid an explosion of flames and swirling sparks, a fifty foot maple came crashing to the ground.

Unfortunately, that had been their escape route—the path that Colin had used to reach the village set. And now it was hopelessly blocked.

Lois looked up at the line of trees from which the actor had emerged. Several of the other maples were bending precariously. It looked as if they might fall any second as well.

Without a word, she grabbed Colin's hand and led him back into the clearing. The smoke was getting thicker, and it was so filled with black soot that the duo could barely see a foot in front of themselves.

They knew they had reached the body of Dorian Hatch when Lois nearly toppled over it. Kneeling beside him, Colin checked for a pulse.

"He's alive!" the actor shouted. Picking up the unconscious director, he slung him heavily over his shoulder.

"Where now?" he grunted.

Lois peered through the smoke and flames, trying to get her bearings. Finally she pointed to the still-unburned edge of the clearing.

"They ran off that way."

Colin coughed and then motioned with his head for Lois to lead the way. She took off in the same direction the two culprits had taken, moving just slowly enough for the burdened actor to keep pace.

Ducking under a low branch, Lois headed swiftly down the path that led away from the clearing. Every few seconds she checked over her shoulder and saw Colin struggling to carry Hatch.

The fire had not yet reached the section of trees through which they ran, and Lois wondered if the worst might not already be behind them. However, as she turned the bend around a cluster of saplings, she realized her hopes were false.

In front of her, the portion of the movie set that served as the village's outer walls and watchtowers was in flames. Lois stopped, giving Colin a moment to catch up.

Through eyes burning from their exposure to the smoke, she scanned the set, looking for Atkinson and Paris.

"Well?" asked a huffing, puffing Colin, as he plodded to a stop beside her. The actor was red-faced with exertion, sweat streaming down both sides of his soot-streaked face. His eyes reflected the savage firelight.

"I don't know!" Lois groaned. "I don't know about Paris or Arlee. I don't see how they escaped!"

Suddenly Colin pointed. "There," he rasped, indicating a ladder that led up to the watchtower and the platform that ran alongside it. The fire hadn't reached that section of the wall yet.

Lois followed Colin's gesture, peering through the smoke and flames. Sure enough, she saw Arlee Atkinson's red hair streaming in the rising wind as the actress picked her way along the platform, just short of the next tower. And in front of her was a figure that could only be Beau Paris.

They evidently hadn't noticed they were being followed—or that they might have pointed out the way to safety, without meaning to. That was fine with Lois.

"Come on," she urged as she headed for the ladder. Colin groaned and followed as best he could.

It took only a few seconds to reach the ladder, and a few seconds more to climb its length to the tower platform. Fortunately this was a functional prop, not just one that was put there for show—or it never would have supported her weight, much less the combined burden of Colin and Hatch.

Once she made it up to the platform, Lois turned and helped Colin. From the look on his face, he needed it. Then, once all three were up, Colin grimaced and lifted Hatch over his shoulders again.

The platform stretched out ahead, toward what seemed like a place beyond the reach of the fire. Lois set her teeth, determined to get them there.

"Just a little farther," she shouted back to Colin over the thunderous roar of the flames.

The platform, unlike the ladder, was not well supported. It shook violently as they moved forward, the fire leaping on either side. What's more, Lois couldn't help noticing tiny tongues of flame working their way upward through the spaces between the planks.

Unfortunately, that wasn't their only problem. Just before Lois reached the next tower, two figures sprang out from inside it.

One was Paris. The other was Arlee. And Paris had a small revolver in his hand.

"Following us, are you?" Paris laughed. "I thought about using this gun to put a hole in our erstwhile director." His eyes glittered fiercely as the flames grew higher and wilder below them. "You know, when no one was looking. Looks like I'll get some use out of it, after all."

"We don't have time to talk," Arlee spat, her eyes slitted with anxiety. "Just *do* it."

Lois swallowed—hard. She eyed the glinting barrel of the pistol. In her heart, she made one last plea for Superman's help, but in her head she was writing her will.

"Yeah," said Paris, his mouth twisting ferociously. "I'll just *do* it."

But before he could pull the trigger, the wind shifted suddenly—and the flames reached up through the chinks in the platform to kiss the end of his cape.

In moments, the whole cape was on fire. Paris screamed and slapped at the flames, trying to extinguish them.

But he didn't accomplish a thing. Desperate to remove the offending garment, Paris dropped the gun and grabbed for the cape's clasp with both hands.

Unfortunately, he couldn't seem to get a grip on it—and Arlee Atkinson wasn't bothering to help. Paris staggered about, flailing frantically as the fire licked at his skin.

And then, to Lois's shock, the man lost his footing. With one last, piercing shriek, he slipped and fell over the side of the platform—into the raging fire below.

Arlee whispered a curse, then looked up at Lois and Colin. To Lois's further surprise, the woman just grinned.

"He knew too much anyway," the actress told them. "This just saves me the trouble of having to get rid of him." Her smile faded. "You two, on the other hand . . . " She shook her head almost sadly. " . . . still present a bit of a problem. Not one I can't handle, of course."

Arlee took two steps toward Lois, forcing the reporter to take a few steps backward to keep some distance between them.

"Look, Arlee," Lois pleaded. She glanced furtively at the fire, which had begun to eat its way into the wooden barrier beside them. "If we don't get out of here soon, we'll all roast."

"Oh, you're getting out of here, all right," Arlee said as she continued to advance. The actress was now next to a stack of metal cudgels, left there for the extras to use in the course of the shooting. "I'm just going to give you a hand."

Arlee grabbed one of the cudgels and held it

140

out in front of her. The actress whirled it like a baton and then presented point forward in an offensive stance.

"That's right," said Arlee. "I was a stunt-woman myself, once upon a time. That's how I met Beau in the first place."

Lois bit her lip. Clearly, the woman knew what she was doing. But the reporter held her ground. If she backed up any farther, she would smack right into Colin and the unconscious director.

They couldn't retreat, either, because the tower behind him had begun to smoke and burn. Nor could Colin put down Dorian Hatch and help Lois defend herself. Unfortunately the platform was too narrow for both of them to stand side by side.

Worse, it was beginning to catch fire. If they remained there, they would die. So Lois did the only thing she could do. She took a couple of steps forward and prayed.

Arlee advanced confidently and swung the cudgel. The blow came at Lois from above. If it landed, the force would almost certainly knock her off the platform to her death.

Fortunately, Lois was able to duck in time. The cudgel whistled harmlessly over her head.

Where was Superman? she wondered. She knew he had lives to save somewhere—but there were lives to save right *here*, right *now*.

Putting the thought of rescue out of her mind, Lois focused on the task at hand. As Arlee swung at her again, she stepped back, out of harm's way—then reached up with her left hand and grasped the end of the cudgel.

As soon as her fingers tightened around the weapon, she twisted it as hard as she could—causing Arlee to cry out and release her hold. Seeing her chance, Lois aimed a blow of her own at Arlee's side.

The pole hit the actress square in the ribs. The impact didn't have enough force behind it to shatter bone, but it did knock Arlee sideways into the wall.

The actress bounced and began to lose her footing. Then she twisted her body gracefully, keeping herself from toppling off the platform and into the flames.

Arlee seemed safe, for the moment—until the flames licking the platform from below suddenly rose up and ate away the last of the platform below her. Screaming, the actress clawed at the surviving planks around her, but it was too late for her to save herself.

Lois lunged to help Arlee, but it was too late. As she watched, horrified, the woman began to fall into the writhing flames below.

Then something happened—something blue and red, moving at a speed Lois's eyes could barely follow. Something inside her cried out for joy.

It was Superman!

Or was it?

CHAPTER SIXTEEN

As Lois peered at the hole Arlee had fallen through, there was no sign of the woman—only the wildly dancing flames. And no sign of Superman, either.

Had she just imagined seeing him? Had Arlee truly fallen to her death? And were she and Colin truly trapped now, even worse than before?

As the flames worked their way toward them, their narrow platform being consumed from either end, Lois cried out in frustration. They had come so close. If not for Arlee's detaining them, they would have made it. Now all three of them—she, Colin, and Hatch—were going to die hideously.

She looked at Colin apologetically. Somehow the actor found the courage to smile, as once his grandfather might have smiled in the original silent *Robin Hood*. It made her smile, too, despite everything.

He started to say something—but any words he may have spoken were drowned out by the crunching, creaking, shattering noise made by the last bit of platform as it splintered beneath them.

Lois braced herself for the end. However, gravity refused to take over and allow them to plummet to their deaths. Somehow, they not only didn't fall, but felt themselves rising.

In fact, it felt like they were flying. Lois unclenched her teeth and found herself safe in the arms of the man she loved. What's more, he had Colin and Hatch as well, and was ascending with all three above the scorched, fiery landscape that had once been Bolt's village.

Lois looked into Superman's eyes. He looked back, his expression conveying a soul-wrenching relief more than anything else.

Then the Man of Steel landed and deposited the three of them on a patch of earth well beyond the ring of fire that had taken hold in the park. As he streaked away once more, flying so fast that Lois couldn't see any more than a blur, she sighed.

It took her a moment to tear her gaze from Superman's departing figure and survey the chaos that swirled all around her. The Metropolis Fire Department had dispatched a fleet of emergency fire-engines to the scene, but the fire was now out of control.

The firemen were putting up a valiant fight, pouring water into the perimeter of the blaze, but already Lois could see that a huge portion of Centennial Park had been scorched.

The struggle now focused on keeping the conflagration contained. If it spread any further, half the city might be forfeited.

Two paramedics made their way up to Lois, Colin, and Hatch to attend to the fire's latest victims. Hatch was still unconscious, his condition caused by a violent blow to the base of his skull, and made worse by the smoke and heat from the blaze. Colin was suffering from smoke inhalation.

Just a hundred feet away, Arlee Atkinson was being treated as well. But in addition to a paramedic, a couple of police officers were keeping a close watch on her. Apparently Superman had alerted them to her status as a suspect in a criminal case.

"What about the fire?" Lois asked one of the paramedics.

The man shrugged. "Could go either way," he replied as he wrapped her wrist in cool, wet gauze. "It's tough to say."

"Superman . . . " Lois muttered.

He was the only one who could fight a disaster of this size. Or was it too much for even him?

Superman gazed down at the fire that threatened to destroy the park and part of Metropolis as well, if he couldn't stop it in time. He needed a way to bring water to bear on the problem—but how?

Suddenly he knew.

Flashing over the cityscape toward Hob's Bay, he found the old, rusty water tower he'd used to fill the makeshift pool in Suicide Slum. Tearing it off its foundation for the second time in as many days, he headed as fast as he could for the bay.

* * *

"Look!" cried one of the paramedics.

Lois followed his pointing finger and saw the Man of Steel fly into view just above the tree-tops. He was carrying a huge old water tower. Water sloshed over the top and sides.

When he was directly over the heart of the blaze, he tipped the tower and emptied its contents into the fire. There was a great hissing and crackling. And before the accompanying cloud of steam could reach the heavens, Superman was gone again.

But a few moments later he was back. Then gone. Then back again. As Lois watched, spell-bound, the Man of Steel repeated his effort again and again, several times a minute, killing a little more of the fire each time.

At one point, she noticed Jimmy Olsen on the scene, taking pictures of Superman's struggle. But he was moving around too quickly for Lois to catch up with him, and truth to tell, her own struggles had wiped her out.

The fire was too vast, too powerful to be brought down without a struggle. Time and again, it sprang up again where it seemed to have been extinguished.

But the Man of Steel was as relentless as the blaze was stubborn. And after a couple of hours, he began to get the better of it.

The conflagration began to shrink, to abate. And within a suprisingly short time after that, the city's assembled firefighters had it under control.

146

The mayor was on hand by then, expressing his wish to thank Superman for what he had done. But the Man of Steel was nowhere to be found.

Lois looked around at the park. Just a few hours ago, it had been a hotbed of film production. Now it was a scene of complete destruction.

Several of the trailers had been turned to charred husks in the fire. Most of the filming equipment, which had been inside the village set, had likewise been destroyed. Several cast and crew members were burned—none of them fatally, but seriously enough to require hospitalization.

All because a couple of actors had been too greedy to think about the carnage their greed might cause. Lois shook her head.

And what about her? Hadn't she been greedy, albeit on a much smaller scale? She always wanted Clark to be there for her, both as himself and as Superman. But now more than ever, she realized that he had responsibilities—to himself, to Metropolis and to the world at large—responsibilities that went well beyond Lois and her wants.

More than that, he was there when she truly needed him. That was what was important, after all.

A hand gently touched Lois's shoulder. She began to turn, expecting to see Colin Dunn, the man who had been there for her over two days.

But it wasn't Colin. It was a smiling, worn-looking Clark.

"Sorry," he said. "I—"

Before he could finish, Lois slid her arms around his neck and kissed him. Then, laying her head on his powerful shoulder, she closed her eyes and nuzzled her nose softly against his neck.

The two stood there and held each other in the growing breeze, which was becoming more and more refreshing with each passing moment.

They didn't speak. But then again, they didn't need to.

EPILOGUE

The next morning saw the sun limp into the sky, exhausted. The heat wave had broken, as if in deference to the actual fire that had besieged the city the previous afternoon.

Clark entered the newsroom of the *Daily Planet* at Lois's side. Though they had only been away from the place for a couple of days, it seemed like forever.

"Danish?" Clark asked as they reached Lois's desk.

"And coffee," she added, "if it's not too much trouble. It's been so hot, I feel like I haven't had a cup of coffee in ages."

He shrugged and bent close to her. "I could zip off to France for some European Blend, if you like."

She rolled her eyes. "Whatever is in the pot will be just fine," she responded. She put her purse down on her desk and picked up a pencil. "Besides," she continued with a smirk, "I want to keep you firmly in my sights for a while. If you zip off, you may get—how shall we say—distracted."

Clark chuckled. He was glad they could laugh about it now. For a while there, he had been really concerned.

He turned away to get their breakfast. But

when he returned with the Danish and coffee, Lois was entertaining a visitor.

Colin Dunn was standing next to her, at her desk. Clark paused for a second to listen to their conversation before he approached.

"You really had me fooled," Colin laughed, "but I should have known all along that you were more than just a production assistant."

Lois laughed along with Dunn. "I appreciate the compliment," she said, "coming from a *real* actor."

Colin's smile faded a bit. "What I really came to do," he continued, "was to say thanks for saving my skin."

"We both did our parts," Lois replied modestly. "Thank *you* for giving me the information I needed."

Colin looked at Lois, as if trying to screw up his courage. Clark sympathized; he had often felt that way in front of Lois himself.

"Speaking of clues," he said, trying to sound confident, "I thought you gave me some clues on the set." The actor paused. Clark saw what was coming next.

"I was wondering . . . " The actor sighed. But before he could finish asking his question, Clark sauntered up.

"Here's your Danish," he said, putting the coffee and pastry down on Lois's desk. Clark then put his left foot on Lois's chair and leaned his body close to hers.

"I'm sorry," he said. "Don't let me interrupt."

Colin seemed to get the hint. He sighed.

"I was wondering," Colin asked Lois, "if there were any more like you at home. You know—attractive, intelligent, full of life?"

Lois seemed relieved that she wouldn't have to jilt a nice guy like Colin Dunn.

"Actually," she replied, "there is. I'll see if my sister Lucy is up to dating a rising star."

Colin laughed. "Thanks," he said. "I'd appreciate that. I'll be in touch."

The actor left just as Perry and Jimmy came bolting out of the editor in chief's office.

"There they are," Perry said in a loud, almost boisterous voice.

"Nice of you to join us," Jimmy added with a mock sneer.

"Now, now, you two, since when is the clock so important?" Lois asked indignantly.

"True enough, Lois, true enough," Perry replied in a softer tone.

Both Clark and Lois noticed that Perry's hands were behind his back, withholding something from their view.

"You wanted to show us something?" Clark chided.

Perry ignored Clark's query and instead focused his attention on Lois. "We're all glad you weren't seriously hurt," he said.

"You bet," Jimmy added. "And you did save a few lives there, Lois."

Lois shrugged. "Not as many as Superman," she demurred. She glanced at Clark. "Did I?"

"No," he agreed, "but you were the one to crack the case."

"And that's just how the story reads," Perry said, producing the morning newspaper from behind his back.

There, on the front page just below the big *Daily Planet* logo, was the banner headline SUPERMAN SAVES PARK FROM FEMME FATALE. Under the large type was the by-line "by Lois Lane with Clark Kent."

One of Jimmy's pictures showed a soot-blackened and bedraggled Arlee Atkinson being led off by police, with a row of charred trees in the background. The actress looked none too happy about it, either.

Lois took the paper and scanned the beginning of the story for a moment. Then she turned to Clark.

"That's not exactly how I filed the story," she said, raising her eyebrows.

"I, uh, did a little editing," Clark explained, defending himself. "I knew you were too modest to play up your own crucial contributions. A reporter reports the news—"

"She doesn't make the news," Lois finished with a sigh.

"I still can't believe that Arlee Atkinson was the saboteur," Jimmy commented. "Her career was on the rise. Why burn her meal ticket?"

Clark shook his head. "I guess she figured fame is fleeting. And the size of that completion bond must have been pretty tempting."

"Clark's right," Lois said. "Jimmy's research turned up Dorian Hatch's life insurance policy and his will. Both named Arlee as the primary beneficiary."

"So she figured to score big," Clark continued, "by trashing the movie and bumping off Hatch at the same time. The money from the completion bond would flow through his estate right to her."

"But why'd Paris get involved?" Jimmy asked sadly.

"I suspect he was in love with Arlee all along," Clark speculated. "Plus, she probably promised him a share of the take. But she was undoubtedly looking to frame him all along— thereby eliminating the only witness to her crimes."

Lois picked up her partner's train of thought. "It wouldn't surprise me if she lured him onto the village set so he would die in the fire, covering her tracks."

Clark nodded. "Apparently she had evidence that he'd tampered with the motorcycle, the wolves, and so on—stuff with his prints on it. And of course, a spray can of Mace that would have kept the wolves from killing him. So Paris would take the rap for all the accidents posthumously, and she'd be free."

Jimmy grinned. "But thanks to Lois—and Superman—Arlee's scheme was foiled in the end."

Perry chuckled. He gave his two star investigative reporters a simultaneous pat on the back.

"You two did some great undercover work," he said enthusiastically. "And I hear from my friend at the film commission that you both played your roles so well, you just might have a second career in pictures."

"Really?" Lois asked, apparently interested, if only for a moment, in the prospect of an acting career.

Perry hung onto his poker face for another heartbeat. Then his lips pulled back in a toothy smile.

"Nope." He laughed. "I was just joshing you." He put his arm around Jimmy's shoulder, and the two began to walk away. "Now, son, *that's* what I call *acting*."

Making sure that no one was within earshot, Clark turned to Lois. "You know," he said, "I really wasn't thrilled about the idea of being away from you so much. I hope you'll let me make it up to you."

Lois shrugged. "It's okay," she assured him, favoring Clark with her most loving smile. "You may not always be there when I want you . . . but you're there when I *need* you."

About the Author

When roused from one of his frequent and enduring daydreams of a world where baseball players never go on strike and White Castle hamburgers grow on trees, M. J. Friedman will admit to being the author of nineteen science fiction and fantasy books, among them a great many Star Trek and Star Trek: The Next Generation bestsellers.

When he's not writing—a condition that lately occurs with the frequency of Halley's Comet—Friedman enjoys sailing, jogging, and spending time with his adorable wife Joan and two equally adorable clones . . . er, sons. He's quick to note that no matter how many Friedmans you may know, he's probably not related to any of them.

Also available from BBC Books:

THE NEW ADVENTURES OF SUPERMAN

EXILE

M. J. FRIEDMAN

"With Superman out of action,
we can rule Metropolis!"

Criminal genius, Thaddeus Killgrave, has turned Superman into the carrier of a deadly virus – so deadly that it's capable of wiping out the world's population. As Superman is forced to go into isolation, Killgrave's thieving associates ransack the streets of Metropolis.

Clark Kent and Superman may be out of action. But Lois Lane is working against the clock to save the Man of Steel – and the human race – from permanent exile.

Also available from BBC Books:

THE NEW ADVENTURES OF SUPERMAN

DEADLY GAMES

M. J. FRIEDMAN

"Somebody's out to get me . . ."

Janna Leighton, a beautiful heiress with a social conscience unveils a plan to invest millions of dollars in Metropolis's disadvantaged communities. But as she publicizes these investments with a series of sporting contests, she becomes the target of assassins.

With Clark Kent by the heiress's side, Superman is able to keep an eye out for her, but Lois Lane doesn't like to be left out in the cold – especially when it's Clark who's freezing her out. Pretty soon, Lois finds herself caught up in something almost too hot to handle, playing the deadliest of games.